THE NOSE FROM JUPITER

RICHARD SCRIMGER

20TH ANNIVERSARY EDITION

tundra

TO NERISSA

Paperback edition published by Tundra Books, 2018

Copyright © 1998 by Richard Scrimger

Published in Canada by Tundra Books,
an imprint of Penguin Random House Canada Young Readers,
a Penguin Random House Company

Published in the United States by Tundra Books of Northern New York,
an imprint of Penguin Random House Canada Young Readers,
a Penguin Random House Company

Library of Congress Catalog Number: 2018945299

Library and Archives Canada Cataloguing in Publication

Scrimger, Richard, 1957-, author
    The nose from Jupiter / Richard Scrimger. — 20th anniversary edition.
Originally published: 1998.
ISBN 978-0-7352-6558-5 (softcover)

    I. Title.

PS8587.C745N67 2018   jC813'.54   C2018-903210-3

Design and illustrations by John Martz
Typeset in Plantin

www.penguinrandomhouse.ca

Printed and bound in Canada

1 2 3 4 5   22 21 20 19 18

Penguin
Random House
tundra | TUNDRA BOOKS

ACKNOWLEDGMENTS

I would like to thank Claire Mackay for giving me the initial opportunity to write about a character who has plagued me for years – did I say that? And Kathy Lowinger, for her confidence in me. "Come on in; write a couple of books," she said, before we were properly introduced; and then, "Great, now change this and this," before I'd had a chance to defend my first draft. And my support system: children, parents, agent, copy editor. Who nose what the book would have been without you?

1

HOW'D I GET HERE?

Don't you hate it when everyone in the room is wearing clothes and you're not? The doctor's wearing a dress with a white coat on top, and the nurse has on one of those green uniforms. Mom's wearing her new tweed suit – a bit wrinkled after a day at work and half the night sitting beside my bed – but still, a suit. And me? I have underpants. Period. I had a hospital gown that didn't do up the right way, but they made me take it off. So now I'm wearing dark green Y-fronts and a smile, and that's about it. No, I forgot. I have a bandage on. It isn't doing me much good, modesty-wise, because it's on my head.

The doctor introduces herself. She's new. I forget her name immediately. I've seen the nurse before; her name is Angela. She's okay. The doctor smiles down at me, pokes

and prods for a bit, and lets me put on my gown again.
That's a little better.

"So you're the boy who talks to himself," she says, taking
the laser out of her pocket. All right, it's not really a laser but
it looks like one, and it feels like one. The other doctors all
had them too. "Angela here has been telling me about you."

I don't say anything. She tilts my head and shines the
light in my eye. Ouch. Like a laser.

"What's your name?" she asks.

Doctors have to go to school for a long time. Everyone
knows how smart they are. They sure know it. But they
must think the rest of the world is as thick as a brick
because they ask really obvious questions. I've seen lots of
doctors since I woke up, and every one of them has asked
my name. Some of them asked more than once. And it's
not like it's a tough name to remember.

"Alan," I say. "Alan Dingwall." Don't say it. It's my
name; I've had to live with it all my life. "I'm still thirteen,"
I say.

"Still?"

"Everybody keeps asking how old I am. I'm the same
age I was a couple of hours ago. I'm still in Grade Seven. I
still live in Cobourg. My birthday is still October 16th."
The doctor chuckles. "And my head still hurts."

"Oh, you poor thing." I can't see her, but that's my
mom. Who was the English queen with *Calais* written on
her heart? My mom has *Oh, you poor thing* on hers.

"We want to know how much you remember, Alan,"
says the doctor. "That's why we ask the same questions

2

over and over again. You were unconscious for almost five hours. That's a long time. We've done lots of tests, but some of them were . . . inconclusive."

"You think I have trouble remembering my own name? Or where I live?"

The doctor tilts my head, stares up my nose. The last doctor did this too. What do they think is up there? Then she goes back to my eyes. "How much *do* you remember, Alan? Do you remember the accident?"

"I've tried," I say. "I remember the rain and the mud. And the creek running high. Norbert was running too – I had a cold." I try to take a breath. "I'm still really stuffy. Even stuffier than I was."

"Norbert is a friend of yours?"

"Uh – kind of," I say.

"And then?"

"I don't know."

"What about your other friend?" the doctor asks. "The little dark-haired girl?"

"Miranda? What about her?"

"She's in the report from the Cobourg Hospital. She pulled you out of the river and called the ambulance. Don't you remember?"

I shake my head. Ouch. Funny that I don't remember about Miranda. Not funny ha-ha, funny weird. She doesn't usually walk home from school with me. She takes a bus. Normally I'd remember being with her. And this afternoon she couldn't have been with me. I know that, though I don't remember why.

Drat. It's like there's a hole in my memory, and every-thing about the accident has fallen in – Miranda, the river, the collie dog, everything. I hope I can find them all again.

Wait a minute. Miranda has brown hair, doesn't she?

"I wish I could remember more," I say.

"That's okay. You're lucky to live in Cobourg, Alan. I've been there once or twice. It's such a pretty place, right by the lake. Look to the left. And to the right. Don't move your head. Just your eyes."

I'm happy to keep my head still. It hurts when I move it. "I wonder if I'll ever remember what happened," I say.

"Probably. Don't worry about it. You always wear green shorts?" the doctor asks suddenly.

"Huh?" I say.

"Your underpants. You like green ones?"

"I . . . not really," I say.

"Good. I don't either. And by the way, just for the record, are those green underpants clean, or did you wear them yesterday too?"

"Hey!"

"Just trying to think of fresh questions. I don't like boring my patients." Now she's shining the light in my other eye. I can't tell if she's smiling but she sounds like it.

"I'm not bored," I say.

"Good. Don't look at the light. Look left again. Now how about this – what's the cube root of four hundred and eighty-nine?"

I blink. "I don't know."

The doctor turns off the light. I can see she is smiling.

4

"Good," she says. "I don't know either. I'd worry if you did know."

At that point the door opens and my dad comes in. "Is this the right room?" he asks. He's moving fast, looking worried and important, until he sees me. Then he stops as if he's been punched hard in the stomach. He takes a slow, careful step toward my bed. And another one. "You're awake!" he says.

I smile feebly.

"I thought you were unconscious," he says. "Sorry I took so long to get here. My flight didn't get in to Toronto until midnight, and the cab broke down on the way to the hospital." He notices my mom. "You said he was in a coma," he says.

My mom is beside the window, looking out. I don't know what she expects to see at this time of night. My dad is standing in the doorway. Whenever they're together, which isn't very often, my parents seem to drift to opposite sides of the room. You'd think they were two like poles of a magnet. Like poles repel, don't they? After the divorce my dad's company moved him away from Cobourg – first to Chicago, and then Minneapolis. Now he lives in Vancouver. Drifted right across the continent. Give him another couple of years and I'll have to fly to Thailand every summer to see him.

The doctor goes over and introduces herself to my dad. I miss her name again. "Congratulations, Mr. Dingwall," she says. "Your son is going to be okay. He was in what we call a light coma, but he came out of it earlier this evening."

"Great," says my dad.

Angela the nurse is holding my hand. Like I said, she's nice.

"Can I go to sleep yet?" I ask. I've been trying to get to sleep since I woke up – that doesn't sound right, does it, but I woke up a little after dinnertime and I've been yawning and yawning ever since. And they haven't let me go to sleep for more than an hour at a time.

"Do you want something to drink first?" asks the nurse. "Some ginger ale or juice?"

"Oh yes," I say. "Please." I'm thirsty. And sleepy. And I have a headache.

Better than being in a coma.

My dad insists on staying with me. I wonder if he really wants to, or if he's just trying to get my mom upset. She wants to stay with me too. "You look awful, Helen," my dad tells her. "Why don't you go home and get some rest? I'll sit up with Alan." And the nurse and doctor smile, like we're a TV family where everyone cares. What we need is a dog, or maybe a pesky little sister. And a crazy neighbor who drops in during every episode.

"You look pretty lousy too," she says.

"Not as lousy as you. Your hair's a mess."

"So is yours. And you spilled something gross on your shirt. Gravy, or something."

"Yeah, well, I was in a hurry."

"And you still turned up too late."

"Too late for what? To see my son in a coma? And anyway, I can't change the airline schedule. I came as fast as I could."

A family fight; not the first one I've ever heard. Looks like we'll have to cancel "The Dingwalls" in mid-season. Parents – who needs them? The doctor and nurse are edging toward the door. I wish I could go too.

"Look, I've traveled three thousand miles to see my son; I'd like to spend some time with him. Is that too much to ask?" My dad is sounding reasonable. A business voice. His job is in human relations. Mom's a social worker, counsels kids in trouble. Ironic, or what? Like that old proverb where the shoemaker's kids go barefoot, and the baker's kids are hungry, and the candlestick maker's kids are in the dark. Nowadays, instead of candlestick makers, we have managers and co-ordinators and directors, and their kids are unmanageable and unco-ordinated and lacking direction. Sometimes I think Lizzie Borden had the right idea.

"Why don't we ask Alan?" says my mom.

"Yes, let's ask Alan. Let's ask him if he wants to spend a few minutes with his old man, who has flown across the continent to be with him. Let's see if a twelve-year-old boy has more sense than his thirty-nine-year-old mom."

"He's thirteen. Don't you even know how old your son is?"

"So I guess you're forty, then. Unless you skipped another birthday. You were twenty-nine for three years in a row, I think."

"I was waiting for you to buy me a birthday present. It took you three years to remember."

But by then I've nestled down into the pillows, and closed my eyes. Maybe they'll leave me alone if I pretend to be asleep.

My dad wakes me up. There's no one else in the room. It's later, I can tell. He's trying to be gentle, bending over me; his face all screwed up. "Alan," he says, shaking my shoulder. "Alan." He looks like he's in as much pain as I am.

"What time is it?" I ask.

"A little after four o'clock." He sounds apologetic. "I didn't want to wake you, but they insisted. They're still a little worried about you."

I don't say anything.

"No, don't go back to sleep. You're not supposed to go right back to sleep. Sit up and talk for a few minutes." He helps me sit up against the pillows. My head hurts.

"Where's Mom?" I ask.

"She went home. She'll be back in the morning." Cobourg isn't that far from Toronto. About an hour by car or train . . . only fifteen minutes by helicopter, which is how I came yesterday. Cobourg Hospital to the Hospital for Sick Children in Toronto. I bet it was a really great trip. Too bad I was unconscious at the time.

Dad goes to the window, stares out at the night. Just like Mom did. Must be a great view from my room. When I can stand up, I ought to go over and take a look. "Alan, I want to say . . . I'm sorry for that scene when I came in the room. Your mother and I . . . we just . . ."

"Yeah," I say.

"I don't know why it is," he says, "but whenever the two of us get together we act like . . ."

"Act like spoiled brats," I say sleepily.

He turns around, laughs. "Yeah, that's about right."

Dad's like me in coloring, very pale and with bright red hair. Now he's blushing. Our blushes are sudden and spectacular, like tropical sunsets.

"I'm going to get myself a cup of coffee," he says. "Can I get you some juice or pop or something while I'm up?"

"Sure," I say. I settle back against the pillows.

"Don't fall asleep. You're supposed to stay awake for five minutes every hour."

He goes.

There's a bed across the room, but it's empty. I'm all alone. I listen for the nurses, for the doctors, for the maintenance staff who push those trolleys around – trolleys which must by some sort of hospital law always have one squeaky wheel. Nothing. Silence. I yawn some more.

I think about my dad in his office in Vancouver. And then the phone call – harsh, dramatic. His son is in the hospital. In a coma. He leaves in a hurry. He's worried because he cares about his son. Because he loves his son. Doesn't he? Well, doesn't he?

I sigh. And hear a familiar, squeaky voice.

– *So, Alan. I guess this is it*, says Norbert.

2

SOMETHING DIFFERENT
ABOUT MY NOSE

"Oh, hi," I say. "Haven't heard from you in a while."

– *I've been busy.*

"I thought you were in a coma too. Did you know that I was in a coma?"

– *No, really? I was in the garage.*

"Say, what happened, anyway? How did I get knocked out?"

– *How should I know? I'm not a doctor.*

"You were there, weren't you?"

I'd better explain. My nose's name is Norbert. No, that's not right. Norbert lives in my nose. He's from Jupiter originally but, for the past little while, he's been staying with me.

I know what you must be thinking – there are times

when I think I'm crazy too. Poor Alan, no wonder the doctors keep asking him how old he is. But other people can hear Norbert too. Angela the nurse came in this evening with a really funny expression on her face, and asked me whom I was talking to. "Your mom is down the hall at the nurses' station," she said. "There isn't anyone else in the room, is there?"

"No one," I told her.

"I was standing outside your door, and I heard this squeaky voice. Were you talking to yourself, Alan? It really sounded different from your voice." I smiled. "Are you feeling all right?" she asked.

Norbert landed one afternoon back in September while I was cutting the grass. An unexpected, uninvited guest. He unpacked his stuff, and he's been with me ever since. As he said when he moved in – *It's a big place, your nose. There's a back room, a kitchen and bathroom, and a garage.* I still have trouble understanding this. But my nose wrinkles up the way it used to, and, when I blow it, the stuff on the Kleenex looks familiar.

"What's in the garage?" I asked Norbert.

– *A spaceship! How else do you think I got here?*

My dad comes back with a nurse. He's got coffee for himself and a can of ginger ale for me. The nurse takes my pulse and temperature, and goes away. My dad falls asleep sitting in his chair, halfway through his cup of coffee. It's quiet in the room. I ask Norbert what he's been doing in the garage.

– *I'm almost finished*, he says.

'Almost finished what?' I wonder. I wonder if everything's okay in there. He's been awfully quiet ever since I woke up. I've hardly been able to get a word out of him.

I think back, and that makes my head hurt.

Memories. One of the doctors told me not to worry, that my short-term memory would return if I just relaxed and gave it time. But it bugs me that I can't remember what happened to me at the river.

"How did I fall in, Norbert?"

He doesn't answer.

"Was Miranda with me? Was that how come she was there to save me?"

He doesn't answer. I'm tired. I fall asleep.

When the nurse wakes me up, it's morning. The thermometers and blood pressure gauges are all busy, and wheels are squeaking on all the trolleys. The nurse changes my bandage, takes my temperature and blood pressure, and asks if I'd like breakfast. I would. I haven't had anything to eat since yesterday – unless you count that bag of clear stuff going into my arm – and that doesn't taste like much, let me tell you.

My dad wakes up with a start. When he sees me he smiles and stretches, then stops smiling when my mom comes into the room. She looks like she slept in a chair too, but she's changed her clothes and put on makeup. My parents don't say anything to each other.

"Do you want some help going to the bathroom?" the new nurse asks me. Like I'm a baby. But when I sit up – not stand up, just sit up straight for the first time in a long time – my eyes swim and my head decides to do a complicated figure-skating jump – a triple something or other – and I fall back against the pillow.

"Oh you poor thing," says my mom.

Yes, I do want help going to the bathroom. And you know what? I'm not even embarrassed, at least not until the nurse stares down at the kidney bowl and says, "Good for you!" Then I blush a bright, neon red and try to disappear under the blanket.

The doctor is pleased with me. "You know, Alan, I really think there's nothing wrong with you. If it weren't for the MRI, I'd let you go home right now."

"MRI?" says my dad.

"Don't you know what an MRI is?" asks my mom.

I remember. I had one last night, as soon as I woke up. It's kind of scary, getting an MRI. They strap you onto a stretcher and slide you into this big sewer pipe, which takes pictures of what they call "soft tissue." Sounds like my friend Victor's rear end. Or his head. Anyway, it's stuff the X ray misses. They spent most of their time around my head and neck, checking for brain function. I asked if they'd found any, but they didn't answer.

The doctor explains all this to my dad who says, "What's wrong with Alan's MRI?"

The doctor spreads the picture against the big lamp beside my bed. "See here," she says. I turn my head. My dad frowns. "What is it?" he asks.

Good question. The picture looks like a satellite weather map.

"This," says the doctor, "is Alan's nasopharynx and sinus cavities – the area behind his nose."

"And there's something wrong with it?" says my dad.

"Let's say, something different," says the doctor.

I feel a sneeze coming on.

"Something bulky and oddly-shaped must have got in the way of the scanner," the doctor goes on. "There are a couple of these projections – whatever they are. The technician says she's never seen anything like it."

"What could they be?" asks my mom.

"Well, I'm no expert. It's probably a fault in the machine. But they look almost like . . ."

"Yes?" My dad sounds worried.

"Well – a spaceship. There, do you see?" The doctor laughs. My parents both laugh. I sneeze. The doctor wants to keep me under observation for a little while longer. If I keep improving, I can go home this afternoon.

"What about his nose?" asks my mom.

"I can't find anything wrong with his nose. He's not running a fever. There's no infection. He looks like a normal, post-concussion patient. I certainly don't want to perform an emergency exploratory operation on someone who's recovering nicely."

"Operation?" I say. "On Nor – I mean, on my nose?" Norbert doesn't even squeak. Maybe he's fainted.

The doctor comes over, takes my hand. "No," she says. "No operation. I want you to relax for a few more hours – chat with your parents, watch TV, maybe take a little walk. And, if you feel like it, try to remember what happened yesterday."

"I've tried. I can't even remember walking home from school. Not really."

My mom pats my hand. "Oh you poor thing," she says.

The doctor comes around to the other side of my bed. "Do you like jigsaw puzzles, Alan?" she asks.

I shrug. Not really. Mom and I used to do them. She's one of those people who can see that the piece has to fit *this* way. I'd be busy trying to fit bits of the sky into the flowerbed, or the windmill, or the castle moat. And what's the point of a jigsaw puzzle, anyway? What do you do when you're finished? Do you admire it like a painting, or play with it, or use it? No, you take it apart.

"Well, right now yesterday is like a jigsaw puzzle with a few holes in it," says the doctor. "A few missing pieces. Right?"

I nod.

"Approach yesterday like a puzzle. Start with what you do remember. Start at the edges of the puzzle, and work inward. Sort your memories like puzzle pieces. Put them together bit by bit. Soon you might have a picture you recognize."

"What if I can't?" I ask. "What if I work and work, and I can't put them together? What if some of the pieces of yesterday are lost?"

I must sound scared because she smiles reassuringly. "That's okay. Don't worry about it. They'll probably come back later, on their own." Probably.

"Where do you want me to start . . . yesterday morning?" I ask.

"Wherever you like," says the doctor.

A trolley squeaks its way into the room. Stacks of plastic trays. "Breakfast for Dingman," says the guy pushing it. I tell him my real name. He shrugs. He's got a floppy shower cap on his head so he won't contaminate my food and drink. Actually, just drink. My breakfast is a gloppy, yellow milkshake. The doctor screws up her face at the sight of it. "That looks awful," she says. "And probably tastes even worse. Orderly, can we find this boy a snack? And for lunch he'd like some real food. Right, Alan?" I say yes.

The shower-cap guy frowns. "But doctor, I just handed in my lunch forms," he says.

"Change them," she tells him.

"You want me to go through all the forms, just to change Dingman's lunch?"

"That's right."

The orderly sighs heavily.

"Dingwall," says my dad. "Not Dingman."

The orderly sighs some more.

"Oh you poor thing," says my mom.

16

An hour later my parents are snoring. My breakfast tray has been taken away empty, and I have gone to the bathroom, so I'm empty too. I went all by myself, which wasn't nearly as easy as I expected. Not a straightforward proposition, if you follow me. Anyway, I'm okay now – which is a step up from last night. I'm thinking about the doctor's suggestion. I wonder where I should start remembering.

I can picture Miranda smiling at me. That's easy. And the soccer game. And the assembly. And the fight in the bathroom afterward. After that, things start to get blurry. "I was walking home along King Street," I mutter to myself. "A gray afternoon. Yesterday? Was it only yesterday? Victor was scared to come with me, so I was all by myself."

– I think you should start the day I arrived.

"Oh, hi, Norbert. I thought you were asleep. Have you been listening?"

– You remember the day? In the backyard?

"How could I forget? But that was weeks ago. I'm not going to start way back there."

– Why not? Haven't I changed your life? You were bored, upset, lonely. A real loser.

"Thanks," I say.

And then I came. Think of that. The Coming of Norbert.

"Sh," I whisper. I don't want to wake my parents.

– Who beat up the bullies? Who introduced you to Miranda? Who scored the winning goal against the Cougars?

"Not you."

– Yes I did!

"Sh," I whisper again.

– Think about it. The Coming of Norbert was the most important day of your life. Wasn't it? Wasn't it!

"Sh!"

Have you ever won an argument with your nose? Didn't think so.

3

THE COMING OF NORBERT

The bell rang, separating silence from noise. Before the bell, the classroom was hushed. The kids were bent over desks, concentrating. After the bell was pandemonium. Friday afternoon – time to stretch your cramped muscles, time to put away weekday anxieties and spend two days thinking about nothing much. So why was I so grumpy? You'd think I wanted to stay in school.

"Walk you home?" Victor called from the desk ahead of mine. "Great afternoon for a walk. We won't even need our jackets." He had a smile on his face. He liked home.

Maybe that was it. I wasn't looking forward to going home. Partly because it was so darned quiet at home. Just me and the dust balls under the TV cabinet until my mom got home from work at six. I nodded to Vic. Sure, I'd walk home with him.

Miranda was looking at me. She was one of the nicest kids in the class and, by far, the best athlete. Smart too, and pretty. Looks like she eats lots of fiber and does push-ups every morning. No reason for her to notice me. Not me, boring old Alan Dingwall. I ate potato chips and generally had no idea – I mean *no* idea – what was going on in math class. Mr. Duschene might as well have been talking a different language. Sanskrit, maybe. I tried to smile at Miranda, but by then she had turned away.

Victor was right; it was a lovely afternoon. Late September – the sun was shining hard and hot. It was like summer, only somehow more precious than summer because you knew it wouldn't last. More precious and sadder. We tied our jackets around our waists.

The bullies from class 7L were hanging around the south end of the school, so we left by the north gate. The Cougars, they call themselves – kids my age who happened to be bigger and tougher than I was. Actually, Prudence wasn't bigger. She was smaller.

There are two gates into our school yard. Every afternoon the Cougars hang out at one of them. Sometimes north, sometimes south. And everyone else goes out the other one. That day we all left by the north gate because the Cougars were at the south one. It meant a longer walk home, along Elgin, but I didn't mind.

Actually, that's not true. I did mind. I minded a lot.

I minded not having the choice to go home the way I wanted. I minded having to do what the bullies wanted. I minded not mattering. The bullies weren't doing this to terrorize *me*, Alan Dingwall, or my friend, Victor Grunewald. Or any of the other kids who walked home. It wasn't personal . . . it was all of us. None of us mattered.

I minded not being able to do anything about it too. What could I tell my teacher, Miss Scathely? Or the principal? The bullies don't threaten us; they don't beat us up or take our lunch money. They don't hurt any of us. But they could. They're mean enough.

Once last year Gary, one of the Cougars, tripped over a kid named Cecil and fell in the mud – an accident. Cecil apologized and everything, but Gary's pants got all dirty. The next week Cecil came to school in short pants. When asked how come, he started to cry. Turned out *all* his pants were dirty. The bullies had waited until wash day, and then taken every pair of pants he had off the clothes line, and dipped them in black paint. And then hung them back up.

To me the scariest part of that episode was the bullies following Cecil to his home. A guy's backyard is his castle; I'd hate the idea of them hanging around where I lived. Cecil and his family moved during the summer. I don't think the paint episode had anything to do with it, but you never know.

Last week a new kid walked past the bullies. It was her first day, and she didn't know what she was doing. We watched her, all of us standing there in the middle of the playground watching this kid from out of town – a Grade Sixer, not big and not small, just a regular girl – walk out the gate past the Cougars. They let her go. They didn't even look at her. They looked at *us*. She walked down the street, all by herself. *And none of us followed her.* We all turned and walked out the other gate. She probably thought we were being snooty, but we weren't. We were just terrorized.

The next day the kid knew better. Somebody in her class told her. From then on, she has gone out the same gate as the rest of us.

It isn't right – all of us acting like sheep, checking to see where the Cougars were hanging out, and turning in a flock to go out the other exit. Another reason I hated going home.

Miranda doesn't act afraid of the Cougars. Mind you, she goes home on the bus.

I stared across the sunny school yard at the Cougars: Larry and Barry, Gary and Big Mary. And Prudence. The rest of us wheeled away from them, heading slowly but inevitably toward the other side of the school yard.

Larry and Barry aren't typical bullies. They're big and dumb, and laugh when someone belches. In a regular class they'd probably get called Moose. But in a class with real bullies – in the same class as Gary, say, or Mary, who laugh when someone gets hurt – they act like bullies too. And, of course, everyone in the class defers to Prudence, who never laughs at all.

Mary is crude; a playground supertanker, sailing on a sea

of snot and dirty words. And gas – I don't envy whoever sits behind her in class. Prudence is an odd one – at first glance, you wouldn't think she belonged on the same school yard as Mary. She doesn't look nice, exactly, because she never smiles. But she could be nice looking. She's small and thin, with a pretty face, I think. She's tidy – hair in a braid, nice clothes. When she spits, she doesn't get any on her. What she is, she's tough. Inside and out. If you did anything bad to her, she'd get you back, even if it killed her. If you knocked her down and then moved across the continent, you wouldn't be able to rest easy. Someday, maybe not this week or next week but someday, you just knew that Prudence would find you and knock you down. And then stomp on you.

And she's strong. Once at recess, I saw her squeeze a can of beans until it burst. Some kind of bet with Gary. There was a crowd of us. The metal of the can cut into her hand so it bled, but she kept on squeezing and never changed expression until the beans erupted out of the end of the can. Then she nodded at Gary and walked away, blood dripping from her fingers.

"Wouldn't it be great if we didn't have to worry about the bullies?" I said to Victor, walking over the Elgin Street bridge. We leaned over. The water was high. Victor wiped his nose. "I don't worry about the bullies," he said.

"We're going the long way home tonight, because of them," I said.

"Oh sure. But I'm not worrying about them."

"It's not right!" I almost shouted. "Don't you see? They shouldn't be getting away with it. We should be standing up to them. I wish I weren't such a . . . such a . . ."

"Coward?" suggested Victor. My friend.

"Thanks, Vic," I said with a sigh. But he was right.

"You don't want to get yourself beaten to a jelly," he said. "Nothing cowardly about that. You're not Superman, just a regular guy."

"Then I need help. We need help. Where should we look for it?"

Victor stared at me. Then he pointed up in the sky. "Look," he said. "Up in the sky. Is it a bird? Is it a plane?"

That Victor. What a riot. I punched him lightly.

"Ow. That hurt."

"Sorry."

He rubbed his arm. "That was a pretty good punch. Maybe you don't need any help, Alan. Maybe you're strong enough already."

I laughed. "Seriously, don't you wish you were seven feet tall," I said, "so you wouldn't have to worry about the bullies?"

Victor shrugged. "If I were seven feet tall, I'd make millions of dollars a year playing basketball. I wouldn't worry about anything."

I sighed. I can't decide whether Victor is the most sensible guy I know, or the thickest.

Turning down the crescent where we both lived, I noticed Victor's mom in the garden. I started to wave, then stopped myself. Victor wasn't waving, why should I? She wasn't my mom.

"What are you going to do when you get home?" he asked me.

"I don't know," I said. I felt kind of mad at myself. I didn't want to watch TV or play on the computer. That'd be too easy. I wanted to punish myself for not standing up to the bullies . . . for not having anyone waiting for me at home. Stupid, I know, but that's how I felt.

"I think I'll cut the grass," I said firmly.

Victor stared at me. He knows I hate cutting the grass. "No, really," he said. "What are you going to do?"

The collie dog didn't seem to have any owner. It hung around, panting and looking at me. "Go away!" I shouted over the noise of the lawn mower, and the dog trotted about four feet away, and relieved herself on one of our rhododendrons. I went back to the lawn. I'd missed cutting it two or three weeks in a row, and it was tough going. I turned off the power, so I could untangle the long grass from the rotor blades. I was thinking about how good a glass of lemonade would taste, when I heard that low buzzing right beside my ear, so close I could feel as well as hear it. You know the sound. So did I. There was a bee nearby. If you can hear it right in your ear, it's too close for comfort. I turned quickly and caught a flash of something hovering right in front of my face – a black and yellow blur about the size and shape of a bullet. I let out a yell and jumped back. The buzzing followed me. I started to run away and tripped over the dog. Stupid thing, probably thought I wanted to play. I stumbled, and the dog and I fell to the ground together. I don't know about the dog, but I got the wind knocked out of me. For a minute or so I couldn't breathe. I lay on the ground in a ball. Finally I was able to take long, excruciatingly painful breaths. "Breathe slowly," they say, "in through the nose and out through the mouth." I heard the bee again, faintly, but I didn't care. I hurt too much. I closed my eyes. 'In through the nose and' – the next thing I knew, I felt a sudden sharp pain.

Yes. *In* my nose. Way in.

I don't know if you heard the story about the bee that flew up the guy's nose, and kept going, crawling and buzzing right into his brain, and stinging him, and he died? Did you hear that one? And when I felt the pain in my nose, that's what I thought about, and I panicked. Hey, wouldn't you?

I blew my nose as hard as I could, holding my other nostril to force the air out of the blocked one. No Kleenex around, but this was not the time to be worrying about manners. After a minute I stopped. Pretty messy, but I didn't care. Was the bee gone? I couldn't see it. Or hear it. Maybe it had flown off to look at the flowers. Maybe not. I blew some more.

My nose didn't hurt.

I didn't know whether to be worried or not. I was pretty sure I'd had something in my nose, and pretty sure I hadn't blown it out . . . but my nose didn't hurt. Not at all. Somehow I figured that if a bee was inside me, I'd feel it.

The collie, meanwhile, had moved a few feet off and was staring at me with her head on one side, like I was a circus act. Stupid dog.

I started to sneeze. I sneezed and sneezed and sneezed. Finally, about twenty sneezes later, I stopped. I couldn't feel anything. I sniffed a few times, experimentally. Still no feeling.

Fine. I must have dislodged the . . . whatever it was. I went back to the lawn mower. That's when I heard the voice.

– *Here we are at last,* it said.

I looked over my shoulder to see who was talking, but somehow I knew there wasn't anyone there. The squeaky voice was coming from inside me. Inside my nose.

– *Ah, this is nice. Say, this is a great place you've got here.*

"Hello," I said. "Who are you?"

– *Living room, bedroom, kitchen, back room. And a garage, of course. Very nice indeed. I think I'm going to be happy here.*

"What are you talking about?" I said.

– *If you could see the place I was living on Jupiter, this . . . this is luxury. Just like the commercials you people send out. This is the life. Ah.*

"That's my nose you're talking about," I said. "Isn't it?"

– *You tell me. I'm a stranger here myself.*

A high and squeaky voice, coming from inside my nose. Suddenly I panicked. I didn't like the idea of something alien living inside me. I had to get it out. I made a fist and hit myself in the nose. Ouch. I held my breath and blew out as hard as I could, one nostril at a time. I screamed and hummed and ran around the backyard, shaking my head. I must have looked like a horse being driven crazy by flies. The dog thought the whole thing was a game. Chased me around the yard, barking and jumping up.

I stopped running. Panted. The dog panted. We stared at each other. Silence.

Could it have worked? I didn't feel anything inside me. "Hello?" I said, very tentatively, hardly daring to hope.

– *Whew! Is it hot in here or is it me? I hope you've got air-conditioning. The last place I stayed at, all they had were these little fans and let me tell you . . .*

That did it. I sat down and started to cry. The dog barked in my face. I tried to shoo it away but it wouldn't budge. I cried harder than ever.

– *Hey, stop that, Big Fella. You're drowning me. Leaking all over the back room here.*

I stopped in surprise. I'd never been called Big Fella before.

– *That's more like it.* The squeaky voice sounded encouraging, before turning tough.

– *And you, Lassie! Go home. Yes, you – go home already. Chase a stick. Or go and save somebody from drowning, okay, girl? Do me a favor. Geez!*

I had to laugh; the look on the dog's face was so comical. After a moment, it shook its head and trotted off.

– *That's better. Laughing is a good sign. Maybe you don't need as much help as you think, Big Boy.*

"Help?" I said.

– *Sure. Didn't you ask for help?*

I didn't answer.

– Well, don't worry about it. I'm going to the kitchen here to put on a pot of cocoa. On Jupiter, we all drink cocoa.

I looked around. None of the neighbors were outside, thank heavens. I didn't want anyone else to notice me talking to myself.

– Don't be so standoffish. I'm just trying to get acquainted. Say, what's your name?

I didn't think I was crazy. Crazy is when you don't know what's going on. I knew all right; it just didn't make any sense. "I'm Alan," I said, and almost stuck out my hand before I remembered there was no one to shake it.

– I'm Norbert.

"And you come from Jupiter," I said. "That is so weird."

– What's weird? You come from Earth. Now that's weird, if you like. A tiny little planet that's mostly water. One thing I will say, though. You're a great host, Alan. I love this place.

"That's inside my nose you're talking about."

– Whatever. It needs a little fixing up, maybe, but there's a lot of potential here. You don't know what you've got inside you, Al.

4

SETTLING IN

I didn't finish cutting the lawn that afternoon. Somehow the urge had gone. I was too . . . I don't know . . . too stunned about what had happened. Also Norbert wouldn't leave me alone.

– *What are you doing?* he kept asking. *What's that? A bicycle? A mailbox? Why are you taking your shoes off on the mat? Are those stairs? Is that a kitchen sink? Is that a real toaster?*

"Yes," I said. "That's a real toaster." And then, to satisfy him, I made toast. He was thrilled.

– *Smells good*, he said.

"Tastes even better."

I had to ask him. "Norbert?" I still wasn't used to talking to myself. We were in the living room and there's a mirror over the mantel and I saw myself in it – an odd picture. "Norbert," I said, "how is it that you speak English? Don't tell me they speak English on Jupiter."

– *You're forgetting about your signals. Sound and light. Radio and television pictures. You've been sending them out for years and years, and let me tell you, on Jupiter a year is a long time. I speak lots of languages.*

"Wow." Cobourg is a little town; there are a few farmers who speak Dutch, but everyone else's idea of a foreign language is the French side of the cereal box.

– *My favorite signals from Earth are the ones broadcasting country music. That k.d. lang is great, isn't she? Do you like her?*

"I don't know. She's not bad, I guess."

– *On Jupiter, we love k.d. lang.*

Dinnertime was usually pretty quiet. Just the two of us, Mom and me, and something warmed up in the oven. That night it was supermarket pizza. Mom was munching hers and reading some reports from work, and I was munching mine and flipping the pages of a Silver Surfer comic when, all of a sudden, I felt a tingle in my nose.

– *What is that stuff you're eating?*

I shot a quick look at my mom. Had she heard?

"Pizza," I whispered.

– *Is it supposed to smell like this?*

"Well, it's not great pizza. But the smell is about right."

Norbert was silent for a moment. I went on eating. I hadn't decided on what to tell Mom about Norbert. I knew I'd have to say something, but I didn't know what. I was kind of hoping he'd keep his mouth shut around other people.

Some hope.

– *Good evening, madam*, Norbert said.

Mom looked up at me. I blushed. She went back to her reading.

– *Nice to meet you. I'm Norbert.*

Mom didn't say anything.

– *Who's the sourpuss?* Norbert asked.

I covered my mouth with one hand and spoke quietly. "Sh," I whispered with my mouth full. "That's my mother."

– *Your mom, eh? You've got my sympathy.*

"Yes, dear?" Mom still didn't look up.

– *She looks like she hasn't had any fun in awhile.*

"Sh," I whispered.

"I beg your pardon," she said. "Did you say something, Alan?"

"No, Mom," I said, truthfully enough. She went back to her report and I – well, Norbert – sniffed hard. I sniff because I'm about to sneeze. Norbert's sniff was pure disgust.

– *Hey, lady! I'm talking to you.*

Oh boy. She looked up with a frown. I didn't know what to do. My face was bright – and I mean bright – red. The blush of the Dingwalls in full flower. I bet I was the exact same color as the tomato sauce on my pizza.

"Did you say something, dear?"

"Um, no," I said. "I think I'm about finished my dinner. May I be excused?"

She nodded grimly. I ran out the door. In my room I sat down and had a chat with . . . well, with Norbert. I suppose it looked like I was having it with myself. Pretty funny.

"Norbert, you can't go around yelling at Mom. It's not polite."

– *Not polite? What about her? Madam High and Mighty. The priestess with the leastest. Is it polite to ignore your own son at the dinner table?*

"That's not fair, Norbert. She talked to me when she got home from work." I felt odd, saying this. My mom isn't rude exactly, but, well, I am her son, and she doesn't spend a lot of time with me. I know she loves me and all, but somehow . . . well, anyway, what I'm saying is that part of me could agree with Norbert.

– *Right. She asked how your day went. Then she said, "That's fine." And then she put the frozen pizza in the oven.*

"She works hard," I said.

– *Does she?*

"She sure does. It's not easy to care about your work and bring up a teenager. And it's not like my dad is around to help." I didn't believe it, I was defending my mom.

– *Uh huh. Well, she's your mom, Big Fella, not mine. Another thing – about dinner. Is it always that bad-tasting?*

"Pretty much," I admitted. "Sometimes we have meat-loaf. Mom makes that. It's good."

There was a knock on my door. "Alan, may I come in?" asked my mom.

I stood up. I don't know why I stood up . . . maybe because I felt guilty. When you're guilty you stand up. I scattered my schoolbooks on my desk to make it look like I'd been reading them. "Come in."

– *We were just talking about you.*

"Sh, Norbert."

Mom came in, staring. "Alan, do you have a cold?"

I had my hand over my nose. "No, no – that is, I don't know. Now that I think of it, maybe I do have a bit of a cold." I pretended to cough.

"It's just that you sounded so strange at the table. And then coming up the stairs, I heard you talking to yourself and I thought . . . I thought you might be sick."

She came over and, a little awkwardly, put her hand on my brow. She's a little shorter than I am now, and she had to reach up. Her hand was cool and dry. She still wore her wedding ring.

– *Say, that smells nice*, said Norbert.

I choked. Mom didn't say anything. She stopped rubbing my forehead for a minute, then went back to it.

– *Very nice. I miss my mom too, you know. She's about four hundred million miles away.*

"There there," said Mom. "Maybe you'd better lie down."

"Maybe I will," I said.

Funny people, moms. My mom knew about Norbert, but she pretended he wasn't there. She didn't really believe in him. She called him my imaginary friend. I heard her on the phone talking to Grandma a couple of evenings later. "Yes, Alan has an imaginary friend now," she said with a laugh. "Just a phase; a lot of boys go through it. The books say it's a sign of creativity. Isn't that nice?"

Norbert sniffed when he heard this, and we went upstairs to do my math homework. Considering he could fly a spaceship and all, he wasn't much better at math than I was. I asked him about it.

– *This stuff is all old math. On Jupiter we're using a new system.*

It didn't take long for Norbert to become part of my life. Partly because I liked company, partly because I had no choice . . . I mean, I couldn't just ask him to leave. By the end of the weekend, I was thinking of him almost as a brother. Sometimes older than me, sometimes younger, but always with a big mouth. Turned out he was older than me, *and* younger. He was three Jupiter years, but it takes Jupiter a bit less than twelve Earth years to orbit the sun. So he was either three or thirty-six . . . sometimes it was hard to say which.

"Why did you pick my nose to land in?" I asked.

– *Well, it was either yours or the dog's.*

I'd forgotten about the collie.

– *You ever been inside a dog's nose? You know where dogs' noses are, most of the time?*

Good point.

I was kind of apprehensive about going to school on Monday. I didn't want to have to explain Norbert to everyone I knew. How could I explain that there was an alien living in my nose? Probably no one would even believe me. They'd think I was the one making the squeaky voice. I don't like to be embarrassed – who does? – and I sensed that somehow, over the next few days, Norbert would find a way to embarrass me.

I met Victor coming out of his house. His mom was on the doorstep. A crisp golden morning, sun rising over the calm lake, sky so blue it almost hurt your eyes to look.

I like Mrs. Grunewald. She's a little, fat lady with an accent like Lucky the Leprechaun. One of the Killarney Grunewalds, she calls herself.

"Bye, boys. Have yourselves a glorious day, now," she said.

"Bye, Mom," said Victor, pulling me away.

"Bye," I said.

– *Farewell, mavourneen!* called Norbert.

Victor turned to me. "What?"

"It's my nose," I said. "He speaks lots of languages. He's very talented."

– *Thank you.*

"What?" said Victor.

I shrugged. I could already feel myself turning red, and I wasn't even at school yet.

5

OR ELSE WHAT?

We got to the school yard just as the bus pulled up to the curb. I've always thought of the school bus as a big yellow sheepdog, rounding up the straggling kids who lived out in the country and delivering them back to the corral every morning. Miranda was the first person off. She lives on a farm – I remember her telling us about it in class – a real farm, with a silo and a barn and everything. They have cows and sheep and a hundred acres of corn. Funny to think of her living in the country and coming into town to school every day. She spends half the week the same way I do, and the other half in a place that's as strange to me as . . . well, as Jupiter would be.

"Hey, guys!" she called out. "Hey, Alan, Victor. Wait up."

I waited, feeling kind of dumb and nervous. I liked Miranda, and had no idea what to say to her. She walked straight up to Victor and said, "Did you have a good weekend?"

Vic nodded.

"Great," she told him, her brown hair bouncing as she bobbed her head. "And what about you, Alan? Anything interesting happen to you this weekend?"

I shrugged. "Not much," I said.

"I'm excited about the intramural sign-up," she said. "Are you guys going to play?"

I'd forgotten about it. Intramural sports – class against class at lunch hour. I didn't like soccer that much.

"I don't know," said Victor. "All that running around."

"Oh, that's too bad." She sounded really upset about Victor not playing soccer. Her face was all scrunched up with disappointment.

"You should play, Victor," she said. "You'd have fun. I'm going to sign up, and I've already talked to some of the other guys in our class. Miss Scathely is interested too."

"Uh huh," said Victor.

We were walking past the tree that stands in the middle of the school yard. It's a pretty big tree, but in bad shape. An elm. The leaves are dry and eaten away. A sick tree. One of these days, they're going to have to take it down. I usually avoid the tree because the bullies from 7L hang out underneath it before school and at lunch hour. A couple of them were there now: Larry and Gary, big guys with flat-top haircuts and tattoos. They were belching at each other – short sharp sounds. They might have been a couple of seals, except that seals don't have such mean expressions.

Miranda walked right toward them. Victor stopped short with a nervous gulp. "Well, um, I'll be seeing you," he said lamely, and headed toward the school.

I wanted to turn away, but I didn't want Miranda to think I was afraid of the bullies. She led me right past them. If I'd wanted to, I could have stepped on Gary's canvas knapsack, which was lying on the ground so you could see the skull picture he'd drawn on it, and read the swear-words. I stepped carefully around the knapsack.

"Watch where you're walking, Dingwall!" Gary shouted. "Or else!"

Now as you know, there are two responses when some-one says "Or else" to you. You can either ignore it, or you can say, "Or else what?" If you're a bully yourself, you can say, "Or else what?" and then go back and step on the knapsack.

I ignored it.

– *Or else what?* said Norbert over my shoulder.

Miranda stared at me. I kept walking, hoping deep inside that they hadn't heard Norbert.

"Hey! Hey, Dingwall!"

They'd heard all right. I kept walking.

– *Hay is for horses!* Norbert called back.

"Shut up," I whispered.

Miranda had her hand to her mouth, like she was hiding a smile. "Gary and Larry are trying to work out what you said," she giggled.

39

"I didn't say anything," I told her. "It was Norbert."

Of course she didn't understand. "That was smart," she said. "Confusing Gary is better than fighting with him."

"It's sure easier," I said. She laughed.

The bell rang. We moved to the Grade Seven lineup, outside the center doors. "Would you think about playing soccer, Alan?" Miranda asked me. "I'd really like it if you played."

– *Of course I'll play*, said Norbert. *Sign me right up!*

"That's great!"

– *For you, I would do anything.*

She gasped. I blushed like a carnation.

"What did you say, Alan?"

"Nothing," I gasped. "Nothing at all."

"I heard you. You and your funny voice, Alan."

"It's my nose," I explained. "He's from Jupiter."

– *On Jupiter, everyone plays soccer.*

She blinked. I liked the smile on her face though. She reached over and tapped my nose with her finger. I liked that too.

– *Hey, you've made me spill my cocoa.*

"Everyone on Jupiter drinks cocoa," I explained. She laughed and laughed.

Nobody seemed ready to believe in Norbert, but he got people's attention all right.

I looked over my shoulder. The bullies were bunched together in line. Gary shook his fist at me. I liked attention from Miranda – Gary's I could do without.

Our cafeteria is small, smelly and noisy. The floor is hard, the chairs are uncomfortable, and the lunch monitor wishes she were somewhere else. Generally I sit over by the window with Victor. Sometimes Nick or Dylan or Andrew will join us – they're kids in our class. We play cards and tell jokes, and try not to listen to what the girls are saying a few tables over.

Not today. I bought some chocolate milk at the counter, and wandered over to our regular table. About halfway through my first sip of chocolate, I looked up to see Mary staring down at me. And Gary. And Prudence. Generally they eat lunch off school grounds, in the field behind the new subdivision, or else they go to the coffee shop down the road. Somewhere they can smoke. The only places to smoke in the school are in the bathrooms, and I guess they don't want to eat lunch in a bathroom. Besides, if you're caught smoking, it's an hour's detention.

Before I could swallow my sip of milk, they sat down.

Victor was just coming in. When he saw what was happening at our table, he walked right by, like he didn't know me. "Hey, Vic!" I shouted. He kept right on walking. What a pal.

The bullies didn't say anything, not even to each other. Pretty odd. "Hi, guys," I said, in what I hoped was a normal voice. "How's it going?"

Nothing. It was going very quietly. Prudence stared at me. She didn't have any lunch. Mary took a huge bite of what looked like liverwurst and onion and cream cheese on a sesame seed bun – a Big Muck, I guess you could call it.

She stared at me with her piggy little eyes, swallowed a huge mouthful, and belched wetly. I wrinkled my nose. The cafeteria smelled bad enough on its own . . . it didn't need Mary's help.

At the other end of the cafeteria, Nick and Dylan and now Victor were sitting with a bunch of little kids – Grade Sixes. I waved at them. They looked away. I didn't exist – as far as they were concerned, I was already a corpse. Dead Man Eating.

The monitor walked past our table. An old lady with thinning hair and thick ankles, she was counting to herself, the way she usually did. Seventeen, eighteen, nineteen, twenty. Number of students in the cafeteria, juice boxes on the floor, days since her last holiday – it was hard to say what she was counting.

Gary kicked me under the table. He wore big fat boots with heavy soles. "Hey!" I said. The monitor stopped, stared at me, started walking again. Twenty-one, twenty-two, twenty-three. I moved my legs out of range.

"Alan, how are you?" asked a familiar voice.

I looked up. Miranda. I was never so glad to see anyone in my life.

"Hey, good to see you," I said. I wasn't tongue-tied at all. I was scared of the bullies. Fear will loosen up anyone's tongue. I sounded like a game-show host. "Why don't you join us? Have a seat," I added, pulling out the one beside me. "Watch out for Gary, though . . . he gets these sudden spastic movements in his legs."

Gary choked. I kept right on talking. "Yes, I've been

having the time of my life with Groucho, Chico and Harpo here. Actually, with Harpo, Harpo and Harpo."

Miranda laughed. Mary and Gary growled like the pair of bulldogs they rather resembled. Yes, I was nervous around them, but the whole scene was funny in a way. I mean, were they going to beat us up in the cafeteria, for heaven's sake? The monitor was ten feet away. The principal's office was right down the hall.

Prudence reached across the table and took my packet of cookies. Too bad, I'd been looking forward to them. "Help yourself," I said. "I hope you like chocolate chip."

All I had left was my apple. I picked it up.

Prudence held the cookies in her hand and slowly crushed them, staring at me the whole time. She dropped the plastic packet on the table. It lay there, hideous and mangled, a poor twisted thing that had once been dessert.

– *That's the way the cookie crumbles*, Norbert commented.

Prudence was startled. Her eyes narrowed. Then she brought down her fist onto the cookie crumbs. Again and again, as if my dessert were one of those Whack-a-Mole games at the midway. The packaging burst, and brown dust scattered all over the table. She must have been really angry, but none of it showed on her face. Kind of scary. I had a bite of apple in my mouth, but I didn't feel like chewing. Miranda put her hand on my arm.

The monitor heard the noise and wandered over. "What's going on?" she asked. She looked irritated . . . probably because we'd interrupted her counting.

43

The bullies stood up. Mary's lunch was all gone. There was a dark stain around her mouth. She licked it obscenely. Prudence leaned over the table.

"You wanted to know, 'Or else what?'" she said softly to me, flicking the broken plastic packet with her fingertip. It spun off the table and onto the floor.

"Pick that up," the monitor ordered. Prudence stared at the monitor, stared at the packet on the floor.

"That's what," she said to me, turning on her heel and heading for the door. Mary and Gary slouched after her.

– *Litterbug, litterbug, fly away home!* Norbert called after them.

The monitor stared at me. "How do you do that?" she asked. "How do you talk in that funny, high voice without moving your lips?"

"It's not me talking," I said.

6

SPORT OF NOSES

My breakfast dishes pile up on my tray. My parents snore in chairs. My head aches under the bandage. It's great to spend time in hospital. So glamorous. And I have to go to the bathroom again.

"What does *mavourneen* mean anyway?" I ask Norbert. I meant to ask at the time but I forgot. Norbert sniffs like he's clearing his throat.

– *It means "my darling" in Gaelic.*

"Why did you call Mrs. Grunewald 'my darling?'"

– *I thought she'd like it, and she did, too. She was still talking about it when we went to dinner last week. She made corned beef and cabbage specially. Ahhh! What a smell!*

"I remember," I say with a shudder. Cabbage is *not* my favorite food. I bet I'm not alone either. I notice that no one has come up with a cabbage-flavored potato chip.

– *Say, what are you doing? You're getting up out of bed. You're not supposed to get up, are you? Rest quietly, the doctor said.*

"I have to go to the bathroom," I say.

– *Do you want to call the nice nurse? Or wake your parents? They could help you.*

"I don't need any help," I say, though the room seems to be spinning very slowly, in clockwise circles, as I lift myself off the bed. Funny, last time I got up the room was spinning counterclockwise. Soccer balls spin that way when you kick them with your left foot. Or do I mean your right foot? Miranda would know.

– *Do you remember the soccer game against the bullies?* Norbert asks. Funny, I was just thinking about soccer. Sometimes it seems like Norbert is listening to my mind. The two of us are really quite close.

– *The one where I scored the winning goal?*

"You did not score the winning goal."

– *Yes I did.*

"Did not!"

– *Did too.*

Like I said, we're quite close, Norbert and I. We agree on everything.

The hospital bathroom is small and clean and brilliantly white. Everywhere I look, I see reflections of the overhead light. Makes my head ache even worse.

The intramural soccer final took place during a dark and yucky lunch hour in November. A crowded noisy school yard, kids chasing each other and falling down, and a couple of bored teachers ignoring everything. The day was cold, and wet, and gray. November. I was standing on the sidelines of the grass field, severely underdressed in short pants and a short-sleeved shirt. I had long socks on, but they kept falling down, and I kept pulling them up, and then of course they fell down again. I wore cleated shoes which I hate. You're supposed to be able to stop and turn suddenly in cleats. All I do is fall down suddenly.

For a variety of reasons, but mostly because Miranda asked me to, I was part of my class's soccer team. The Commodores – Miss Scathely named us. She takes intramural sports seriously. Apparently the Commodores were a music group from her childhood. Good thing she doesn't like classical music, or we'd be the 7A Philharmonics or something.

The game was about to start. Across the field our opponents were gathering. The Cougars. Five of them, like us. Intramural rules. It's more like hockey than soccer, really. We don't have a very big field. With eleven people on a side there wouldn't be enough room left for the referee and the ball.

Miranda called us into a pregame huddle. "Remember what we talked about," she told us. "Don't let the Cougars rattle you. Get the ball downfield fast. Don't dribble it, pass it." She talked some more but I didn't pay much attention. Soccer is not my favorite game. I didn't care

47

about tactics and strategy, and getting the ball downfield and dribbling. I thought dribbling was basketball, anyway. And little babies. I didn't know it was soccer.

Even if I loved soccer, I wouldn't want to play it against the Cougars. They didn't have a pregame ritual. They just piled their leather jackets in a heap, spat out their gum, and stood around punching each other.

Miss Scathely was walking up and down the sidelines, wearing a jacket with COMMODORES on the back. Mr. Taylor taught 7L, the Cougars, but he didn't show up for intramurals. I think he enjoyed the time away from his class.

You'd think a group of bullies wouldn't bother with intramural sports. Why play soccer when they could be playing with knives and matches? It was Prudence's idea to ruin the intramurals for everyone else. Poor Mr. Taylor . . . his hair is a lot grayer than it was at the start of the year. The Cougars had beaten every other team. Now it was our turn.

"Let's go, people!" said the gym teacher, Mr. Stern. He blew his whistle. Miranda trotted up to the center circle. So did Mary the bully. And Larry the bully. And Gary the bully. "Come on, guys," Miranda called over her shoulder to her cowering teammates, me among them.

"You know the rules," said Mr. Stern around his whistle. Before they let you become a gym teacher, you have to be able to talk with a whistle in your mouth. "There'll be two fifteen-minute halves, plus penalty time at the end. Rough play will be penalized very severely." He looked at the bullies as he said this. Last game they broke Andrew's wrist – all an accident, they said afterward, "Gosh, we're really sorry." But I talked to Andrew the next day and he said Mary had done it deliberately – tripped him and then jumped on his arm.

"Is that understood?" Mr. Stern looked at Mary the bully. She nodded coolly and blew her nose onto the grass, one nostril at a time. Then she licked under her nose. I don't know what she did after that because I looked away.

We got the ball first. Miranda passed it to my friend Victor, on the right side. Mary's side. She charged at Victor, screaming for him to get ready to be hurt.

Miranda should be telling this next bit. She knows so much more than I do about the game. As I understand soccer, you kick the black-and-white spotted ball downfield and the other team kicks it back, and then you kick it back at them. At some point the ball goes out-of-bounds and you throw it in over your head – I don't know why you throw it in over your head, but you do. Then there's a bit of a tussle and, suddenly, someone has a shot on goal. And either the ball goes in the net, or it goes wide and the goalie picks it up and kicks it a long way. And then you do it all again. At halftime you change ends. After the game you change clothes.

Miranda has tried to explain the subtleties of the game to me, but I can't remember any of them. Midfielders and strikers and marking your man, crosses and offsides. She gets excited. Her bright blue eyes start to sparkle and she tosses her hair off of her forehead. Her hands move around.

"Uh huh," I say, watching her. At game time I do what I always do, run up and down the field and, if the ball comes to me, kick it to someone else.

Our game against the Cougars looked like all the other games we played, but with one difference. Not obvious at first, it became clearer and clearer as the game progressed. We – the Commodores – spent much more time than usual on the ground. I watched to make sure. Our goalie kicked the ball upfield to Nick, a nice guy with glasses who likes to draw pictures of aliens. Nick had the ball, and Larry was coming to take it from him. Just as Nick passed the ball away, Larry knocked him down. "Hey," Nick called, getting to his feet. But Victor had the ball now, and Mr. Stern was watching him. After Victor kicked the ball away, Gary knocked him down. "Hey," Victor called. But Mr. Stern missed it. Gary smiled down at Victor, spat, and trotted off, tripping Nick again as he went past. "Hey," called Nick.

No question, the Commodores were playing this game from the seat of their pants.

Miranda is a wonderful soccer player. She took the loose ball – I love that phrase, loose ball, as if it's usually prim and proper, and now it's had a couple of drinks and let down its hair – away from Larry, and kicked it right between Gary's legs, then ran around him so fast he fell down trying to trip her. Miranda raced down the side-line, pushing the ball in front of her effortlessly, as fast as I can run without the ball. Her hair flew behind her like a banner. The Cougars all ran after her. I ran too, a safe distance away from them. From the other sideline, Miss Scathely was cheering her on.

Miranda was almost all the way downfield now. There was a single defender between her and the goal. The rest of the team was closing in. The angle looked wrong for a shot. She glanced over her shoulder, and sent the ball looping into the middle of the field. I think that's a cross. Anyway, the ball soared over the heads of the Cougars to land right in front of – you guessed it – me.

Just me and the ball. And, not too far away, the goalie, Barry. Time stood still. I had plenty of time. I noticed that Barry's socks didn't match – one of them had stripes around the top, and the other one didn't. I knew the Cougars were coming. I knew the Commodores were cheering. I didn't hear them. I took a deep breath and felt the field rolling under me, as calm and comforting as an ocean wave. I smiled, and drew my foot back for the shot.

It was the last time I smiled for awhile. No, I did not fall. I was –

– *Yes you did*, Norbert interrupts in a whisper.

"Did not," I say.

– *You did so fall. I remember vividly. I was right there.*

"I didn't fall," I whisper. "I was tripped."

– *You fell. You fell over your own stupid cleats and ended up on the ground with your feet wrapped around your ears. I was humiliated.*

"Norbert, please. Prudence tripped me from behind." The hospital room is quiet, except for the snores of my sleeping parents. And me and my nose, arguing.

– *Prudence was across the field. If she tripped you she'd have to wear size seventy-eight boots.*

I don't say anything but I'm thinking, 'I did not fall.'

– *Did so*, says Norbert.

"All right, all right," I admit. "Have it your way. I fell down."

– *Clumsy oaf*. Norbert doesn't believe in forgiving and forgetting.

Anyway, Prudence ended up with the ball. She kicked it downfield, and Miranda couldn't get back in time, and Gary blasted a shot from about twenty feet out. Dylan is our goalie because he takes up the most space. He's six inches taller than I am, and almost twice as wide. His hair is big and thick, like the rest of him. He made a feeble move with his hand. From my position on the ground, it looked like he was waving good-bye. Didn't matter; the ball was already in the net.

1-0.

Prudence stared at me as I got up. I could feel her eyes on my back as I trotted ashamedly back to the Commodores' end of the field. I apologized to Miranda, but she told me not to worry. "Prudence tripped me," I said.

"Good try," she said. I wonder if she believed me? The ball was in the center circle. "Come on, guys," she said.

"We'll get them this time." Mr. Stern blew his whistle and the game went on.

Nothing really exciting happened until near the end of the half. They kept knocking us down, and we kept saying, "Hey." Once or twice Mr. Stern noticed, and told them to play more cleanly. Once he gave Victor a penalty shot, but Victor missed. They scored again. They almost scored a third time, but by some fluke Mary's shot went right at Dylan and bounced off him to Nick, who kicked wildly in exactly the right direction. The ball flew downfield as if it had wings, right over the heads of the Cougars. Everyone stared up in blank amazement, as if they expected something other than a soccer ball to be flying through the air. A pig, maybe, or a cathedral. Everyone stared up except Miranda. She took off at top speed as soon as the ball left Nick's cleated foot, when it bounced a couple of times and started to roll – the ball, that is, not Nick's foot. Nick's foot was still attached to his leg – she was the closest one to it except for Mary. Mary saw her coming and stuck out her foot, but Miranda leaped over it like a gazelle and took off with the ball toward the Cougars' goal. Seconds later the ball was in the net and Miranda was jogging back.

Once again time slowed down. I saw the look of rage on Prudence's usually impassive face. I saw Mr. Stern put up his hand and blow his whistle to indicate halftime. I saw Gary knock Nick down. Then I noticed my shoelace was undone. Stupid cleats. I bent down to tie it up . . . and it must have happened then. I heard a cry of pain and then a collective "Hey!" from the Commodores. I looked up. Miranda was rolling on the ground, grabbing at her ankle. Prudence stood over her, hands on her hips.

"Did you see that, sir?" Victor ran over to Mr. Stern. "Did you see that, sir? Prudence just kicked her. Kicked her right in the ankle."

Mr. Stern bustled over, blowing his whistle. "What's going on here?"

By then I was beside Miranda. "Can you get up?" I asked, helping her to her feet. She took a step and almost fell down again.

"Sprained, I think," she said. "Not too serious."

"What happened?" Mr. Stern asked her.

"I don't know, sir. Something hit my ankle and I fell over."

For just a second, Prudence looked surprised. She hadn't expected Miranda to say that. Mary laughed out loud. Gary and Larry snickered to each other.

"Prudence kicked her!" Victor pointed his finger. Nick nodded his head so vigorously his glasses slipped.

"Did *you* see?" Mr. Stern asked Miss Scathely, who had hurried over from the sidelines.

"No. There were too many other people in the way."

Mr. Stern frowned his gym teacher's frown. "Well, Prudence? What happened?"

Prudence stared at him, as if he were an insect and she a can of Raid. "She fell down."

Mary added, "Her whole darn team's been falling down

all darn game." Only she didn't say darn. She laughed until she coughed, and then spat vigorously onto the grass.

"Watch your language, Mary." Teachers love an issue they can hang on to.

"Sure, sure." Mary turned away.

Miranda hop-jogged across the field. I ran after her. She was steaming, but not at Prudence. She was mad at herself. "I might have known she'd try something like this. I should never have let that . . . that female dog get so close to me," she said. Miranda doesn't swear.

"Why don't you tell Stern that she kicked you in the ankle? He'll believe you, and Prudence will get sent off. What do you call that – red flagged?"

"Red carded." She smiled. Her smile was twisted, like her ankle.

"Whatever."

"Oh Alan." Miranda likes me but she's not always sympathetic. "What good would that do? I don't want to whine to the teacher because some kid is mean to me. The best thing to do is to beat her. That's what she can't stand. Let's win the game, Alan."

The sun looked out for a second; the day got almost warm. The other Commodores were milling around helplessly. Every now and then they looked over at us. Mr. Stern was blowing his whistle, ready to start the second half.

"How do you feel?" I asked. "Seriously. Can you play at all?"

"Seriously, not too good. I can kick the ball, but I can't run after it very fast."

"And you think we ought to win the game against the Cougars without you? Is that the best plan?"

She nodded wearily. I wondered what the second-best plan might be. Without Miranda, we had as much chance as an ant at a tap dance class.

The whistle blew to start the second half. Cougars' ball. Mary tapped it across the circle to Larry.

And then, without warning, another player made his presence felt.

– *Look out, Larry!* shrieked Norbert at the top of his voice.

7

UP TO ME

Larry fell for it. He looked over his shoulder, stumbled, and inadvertently kicked the ball to me. Before I knew quite what was going on, I was running downfield, giving the ball little nudges with my feet as I went so that it stayed ahead of me, but within reach.

– *This*, said Norbert excitedly, *is called dribbling the ball. On Jupiter we practice this all the time.*

"I've seen kids do it in European TV commercials," I said, panting a little. "Italy, I think it was."

– *Italy must be a lot like Jupiter.*

"I don't think so," I said. Mind you, I've never been.

Heavy footsteps pounded behind me. "I'm going to kill you, Dingwall!" Gary shouted.

– *How? You going to breathe all over us?*

57

"Shut up, Norbert." Gary is pretty mean, and he's a lot bigger than I am.

"Who said that? Was that you, Dingwall?"

"No," I panted. "It wasn't me. I think your breath is great."

What a coward I am, and of course it never pays to be a coward. Gary thought I was kidding, and let out a roar of rage. I heard his footsteps getting louder and louder. Panic-stricken, I kicked the ball. I tried to kick it straight downfield, but it went off the side of my foot by accident. I ran as hard as I could toward the near sidelines because that's where Miss Scathely was. She was cheering. I looked over my shoulder. Gary wasn't following me anymore. He was running after Nick, who had a clear shot on goal. Somehow my errant kick had turned out to be a great pass.

Gary was exhausted from all his shouting and chasing. He had just enough strength to tackle Nick from behind. Mr. Stern blew his whistle and gave Nick a free kick. You know what a free kick is, where the other team stands away from the ball, making a human wall to block the shot. I must say, when Mary and Gary and Larry and Prudence linked arms and stood shoulder to shoulder to shoulder to head (Prudence is a lot shorter than the others), I didn't see how Nick could get the ball by them. Especially as they kept staring right at him, with their mean bully eyes. He's a nervous and sensitive guy, Nick – an artist. Those aliens he draws may have superior technology on their side, but they sure look frightened. He straightened his glasses, took a deep breath, and ran up to the ball.

– *Look, Gary, there's money in the grass. A dollar, I think. Beside your foot!* Norbert sounded excited. Gary couldn't tell where the voice came from. He bent over, and because his arms were still linked to Larry's and Mary's, they were forced to bend over too. Nick let fly just as their heads came down. The ball flew over them like a horse clearing a difficult jump. The goalie, Barry, was distracted too. He was staring down at Gary's foot. The ball trickled by him into the net.

2-2.

"Good shot, Nick. Now get back, everyone." Miranda didn't want to antagonize the Cougars. She wobbled back to our end. Nick followed, looking stunned and a bit apprehensive. Victor patted him on the back.

The Cougars were on the ground, linked together at the elbow.

– *You guys look like a charm bracelet!*

"Norbert – quiet," I muttered under my breath. "You're going to make them mad!"

– *That*, he told me, *is the idea. If they're mad, they'll play badly.*

"Is that how it works on Jupiter?" I was running back to our end as fast as I could. Safety in numbers. I heard the Cougars cursing me in the distance.

– *Actually, on Jupiter we all play nicely.*

I shut my mouth and tried to concentrate on soccer. But it didn't matter about my mouth. I couldn't shut Norbert up. He kept making fun of the Cougars: their hair, their clothes, even their earrings and tattoos.

– *Who's that supposed to be?* he shouted at Gary, who has an eagle on his forearm, just below the elbow. Actually it doesn't look bad; somewhere between cool and repulsive. "Cost two hundred dollars," he boasted, and it might have.

– *It looks like Donald Duck!* Norbert shouted.

Victor grabbed my arm. "Shut up," he whispered. "Stop insulting the Cougars. They'll kill you!"

"I'm not doing it," I said. "It's Norbert."

He looked at me like I was crazy. Maybe he was right, but I caught an admiring glance from Miranda. "My hero!" the glance seemed to say. "My knight in armor! My champion!" She passed me the ball.

"Kick it downfield, Squeaky!" she called.

My Squeaky. Oh well. I kicked the ball as hard as I could.

The Cougars didn't know what to think. They were sure it was me – which is what I was afraid of, and why I spent a lot of time near the referee – but, well, when Norbert talks my lips don't move. It's like I'm a ventriloquist, only of course I'm not in charge. I can't make Norbert say what I want. You'd be closer to the truth if you said I was the dummy.

"You wait, Dingwall," said Mary. "I'll see you after school!"

I shivered with fear, and tried to tell her I was sorry and that it wasn't my fault, but Norbert made a whistling noise.

– *I'll wear a carnation,* he said. – *Just remember, I don't kiss on the first date!*

Even Larry laughed at that. Like I said, he's not a real

bully. I stared at Miranda helplessly. She was laughing. "Way to tell her, Squeaky!" she called.

The game was deteriorating – a lot of pushing the ball back and forth in the center area. I didn't mind. It was easy to keep close to Mr. Stern. Every now and then we'd work the ball to Miranda, and she'd boot it down the field a long way, and all the Cougars would chase after it.

Mr. Stern blew his whistle. "Last minute of play!" he called, looking at his watch. I dodged out of Prudence's way – not the first time I'd had to do this. She'd been following me for most of the half, like a bloodhound on the trail of an escaping convict. Norbert's insults were rattling her team. They were rattling her. His plan was working: the Cougars were playing badly. I was scared. I knew she'd get me some-time. For now I tried to keep her and Mr. Stern in my sight. She tried a blind-sided tackle while he was looking at his watch, but I edged away just in the nick of time.

Speaking of Nick, he was standing still, watching Gary and the ball get closer and closer. He might have been a bird watching a snake. I ran up to help.

– *Pussycats!* Norbert yelled at the top of his lungs. – *You're not Cougars at all! You're just little kitties!*

Gary got so mad he stopped dribbling – that's what he was doing – and shouted back. "Well, you're not a Commodore, you're just . . ." and then he stopped, because he couldn't think of an appropriate insult. Mr. Stern laughed so hard his whistle fell out of his mouth. Good name, Commodores.

61

Meanwhile, Nick darted forward, took the ball away from Gary, and booted it down the field. Gary pushed Nick down, and we all raced after the ball. Guess who was there first? Not me. Not Gary. Not Prudence . . . she was right behind me. Not Nick, of course . . . he was on the ground. Not Mary . . . she was second. The first person on the ball was Miranda. She must have started running even before Nick kicked it. Anticipation, they call it – a very useful quality. The ball was in the corner. Miranda couldn't dribble it anywhere with her bad ankle, so she waited until the rest of us got downfield, and then booted it right in front of the net – a high, looping, crossing pass.

I should have seen the danger coming, but I was too excited with the tie game and the last minute of play and the ball coming down, and all of us elbowing and shoving in front of the Cougars' net. Barry the goalie was getting ready to jump and grab the ball before it landed. I was standing only a few feet away, right in front of the net. I didn't see how I was going to get the ball, though, because Gary was between me and the net, and he's almost a foot taller than I am. I looked around for support. Miranda was still in the corner, hopping on one foot. Victor was on the ground – Mary had knocked him down. Nick hadn't arrived yet. It was all up to me. I crouched down, ready to leap up at the precise moment the ball would hit – and then, with my rear end sticking way out, I remembered Prudence. Behind me.

Talk about being vulnerable. You know those Second-World-War movies in the North Atlantic? Well, at that moment I felt like a munitions ship with a U-boat on my tail, and then Prudence launched her torpedo. Wow. Her right boot, with all her strength behind it, hit me right in the . . . well, let's say in the stern.

Explosion! Next thing I knew I was flying into the air – up, up and over Larry's head – so that when the ball came down it hit me first.

– No it hit me *first.*

Norbert has a point. It hit him first.

– It hurt! I had to go to the back room for a cold cloth.

The ball bounced off Norbert and hit the inside of the goalpost and then, as Mr. Stern blew his whistle to end the game, it hit the back of the net.

3-2.

The intramural championship was ours. We'd get a team trophy and individual ribbons at the next school assembly. Nick and Victor were slapping me on the back. Miss Scathely was jumping up and down on the sidelines. And then, best of all but kind of embarrassing, Miranda hobbled over and kissed me in front of everybody.

– No, she kissed me.

My seat still hurt, but it was worth it.

The Cougars slouched away to lick their wounds . . . actually, to get some more gum before the bell rang. Lunch hour was almost over. Time to change. I was chilly and dirty, and a bit scared of what might happen after school.

Remember the first time you did something you knew was wrong: stayed out too late on purpose, looked at a movie or magazine you weren't supposed to, used your milk money to buy candy, smoked a cigarette, or said a really bad word out loud? And then you held your breath, waiting for the sky to fall?

That's how I felt. I'd insulted the Cougars . . . actually, Norbert had, but they didn't know that. As far as they were concerned, I was guilty. I was the one they were going to obliterate.

The afternoon passed as in a dream. Miss Scathely handed out jellybeans to all the team members, and beamed whenever she looked at one of us.

Mr. Duschene, the math teacher, didn't beam. He didn't hand out jellybeans either. He handed out detentions.

"Express the number forty-eight in base six, Dingwall," he said. I stared at him. Heaven knows what I was thinking about.

"Why would I want to do that, sir?" I asked. The class tittered.

Mr. Duschene frowned. "Because I asked you to, Dingwall," he said.

Victor sits behind me in math. "A hundred and twenty," he whispered. Victor's good at math. His answer might well have been right. It sounded ridiculous, but then a lot of math does sound ridiculous. I didn't understand about the different bases, and how ten is really just a placeholder, so that sometimes six is ten, and sometimes eight is ten, and sometimes twelve is ten.

"Would it help if I told you that thirty-six is a hundred, Dingwall?" Mr. Duschene said.

"Is it?"

"In this case – yes."

I felt like Alice in Wonderland. "Then I'll tell you, sir – it's no good to me at all."

"Come on, Dingwall. You don't usually waste our time with smart answers. Do you understand that thirty-six is a hundred?"

"But sir, a few minutes ago you showed us that sixty-four was a hundred."

"Yes."

"And before that . . . before that *nine* was a hundred."

"Yes." He smiled that math teacher's smile – superior, but tolerant – more in pity than in anger. It wasn't my fault I was stupid. "Any number can be a hundred, Dingwall. In base two, four is a hundred."

"Oh."

Where was something you could count on? Where were the constants in life? Who said numbers can't lie? Here was a hundred, a plain and simple concept, easy to understand – a dollar was a hundred pennies, a sprint was a hundred meters – and this simple number becomes as slippery as a piece of soap. All over the place. And just when you got used to its changing size – there, it's sixty-four – you find out it's really thirty-six. Or eighty-one. Or four. I felt betrayed by something I'd trusted. I was reminded of the day I came home to find that Dad didn't live with us anymore. Something I thought was forever, something I hadn't really thought of as present, was suddenly absent. And my life was changed forever.

My dad . . . a hundred . . . what next?

"So in base two, a dollar is really worth four cents? And Donovan Bailey runs the four-meter dash? Is that right, sir?" The class tittered again. "And that song – 'A hundred bottles of beer on the wall' – has got only four verses? It's just crazy, sir." I put my head in my hands.

From somewhere behind me came Nick's voice. "Way to go, Squeaky!"

The class laughed out loud. I turned to glare at Nick. This wasn't Norbert talking. This was me.

"You can stay after school tonight, Dingwall," said Mr. Duschene. "For a hundred minutes . . . in base five. You see if you can work it out."

Mr. Stern shook my hand in gym class. "I'm so glad you guys won today," he said to Victor and Nick and Dylan and me. "A very special guest is coming to our next assembly. An old alumnus . . . probably our most famous alumnus. He'll present the trophy. I wouldn't want him thinking the Cougars are representative of the best this school has to offer today."

"No, sir," I said. I wondered who had gone on from our school to be famous – no one I'd ever heard of. I asked Victor about it after the last bell.

"Who's the special guest at the assembly?" I asked.

He didn't know. "Man, are you ever going to get it from the Cougars," he said, shaking his head. "You won't live to see the assembly."

Our lockers are side by side. He was stacking his books neatly on the shelf of his locker; largest book at the bottom, smallest at the top. A neat little pyramid. He always does that. I throw my books into my locker. Usually the heaviest ends up at the bottom.

"Well, who's our most famous alumnus?" I asked.

"I don't know – what's an alumnus?"

Good old Victor. He knows so much about some things, and almost nothing about anything else. Ask him about computers and he'll give you chapter and verse. Or sex – I sometimes wonder if he's making it up, but he sure sounds knowledgeable. "An alumnus is someone who went to the school," I told him.

I kept my math book, threw the rest into my locker, and closed the door. Victor was having trouble doing up his jacket. He never gets his clothes big enough. His shirt buttons work a lot harder than mine do. When I asked him why he didn't get a larger size, he said, "Why? I'm not that fat. I can still fit into a medium." Funny, medium only makes him look fatter than he is.

"My dad went here," he said. "Years and years ago."

"Victor, your dad runs the Safeway over on Division Street. I'm talking about someone famous. Someone even you and I know."

He thought for a minute. "But, Alan, we both know my dad."

Victor wasn't getting it. "Someone even more famous than your dad," I said. "Someone on the evening news.

The prime minister or Shania Twain, someone like that."
Though it probably wouldn't be someone like that, or we'd
have heard of him.

"I didn't know that Shania Twain went to school here,"
said Victor. "I thought she was from some place up north."

– *Shania Twain, the country singer?*

"Forget it." I closed my eyes and took a deep breath.
"Just forget it."

– *Shania Twain is coming to this school?*

"Hey!" Victor was calling to some kid down the hall.
"Hey, guess who's coming to the assembly tomorrow!"

The late bell rang. I had to get to my detention. "Quick,
Victor. What's a hundred in base five?" I asked him.

8

FILES DON'T TALK BACK

The Cougars had left the school yard by the time I got out from my detention. I looked around carefully, but couldn't see any trace of them. Usually they left some fresh gum or graffiti to remember them by. I still went the long way home. It was a cold and gray day. It would have been faster to walk home by King Street the way I usually did, but I didn't want to meet Prudence and Gary. I'd have to confront them sometime, but I thought that if I waited long enough, their anger would cool down. Maybe they'd let me live.

There was a lot of dust in the wind. I screwed my eyes shut and bent my head. Norbert sneezed and said he was sorry.

"Fine," I said. I wasn't very happy with Norbert. It was all his fault. He was the reason I was in trouble.

– *I can't understand it,* he said at last.

"What?"

– *Everyone calls you "Squeaky," but I can't understand it. You don't sound squeaky in the least.*

"They do not *all* call me 'Squeaky!'" I protested hotly. "A couple of kids made some remarks. And for your information, they were calling *you* 'Squeaky,' not me."

– *Why would they call me "Squeaky?"* He sounded honestly puzzled.

"Because of your voice."

– *But there's nothing squeaky about my voice. On Jupiter my voice is considered very deep and resonant.*

I didn't have anything to say to that.

– *Though I do think Miranda has a soft spot for me.*

"You?"

– *She kissed me, didn't she? In front of the whole team. Yes, I think she has a soft spot for me, Squeaky.*

I sighed.

It rained hard that evening. I stood in front of the kitchen window watching the water drip off our clothesline, listening to the distant rumble of thunder. Mom was talking on the phone. Evenings at our place tend to be on the dull side. I don't have any brothers or sisters, and Mom spends a lot of time on her work.

I put some cookies on a plate and got myself a glass of milk to go with them. "Cookies and milk make the stomach feel smooth as silk," my dad used to say all the time. Course he also said it about grilled cheese and milk, or coleslaw and milk; whatever he was eating. Mom hung up the phone and went back to work.

"Did you used to play intramural sports in school?" I asked her. We'd talked a bit about the soccer game at dinner.

Mom didn't answer.

"I wonder what the championship ribbons will look like," I went on. "Sometimes they're blue, sometimes gold. I hope they're gold."

Mom made that noise to show that she'd heard me, but wasn't paying a lot of attention. The kitchen table was piled high with case files. I pushed them out of the way, so I could make room for the plate of cookies. Without looking up, she asked me to be more careful.

"They're just files," I said.

She sat straight up. Now I had her attention. She spoke slowly, carefully, angrily. "They're not files – they're human beings. They're not just paper, they're flesh and blood. Each of these cases is a real living, breathing, troubled person. Don't you dare call them 'files' again. You're so . . . insensitive!" It's her bad word.

I wanted to say, "What about me, Mom? I'm a human being too." But I couldn't. I was afraid. I was afraid that the cardboard and paper human beings on the table were more important to her than I was.

Of course they were easier to deal with, in a way. They didn't talk back. They didn't spill cookie crumbs and forget to make their beds and stay out late and use bad words. They were living, breathing people, but they were awful quiet. And they didn't take up much room. And when you were tired of them, you could fold them up and put them away.

I finished my milk and cookies in silence, and went up to my room. The rain came down harder. The wind rose, and I saw the cedars across the road swaying back and forth. There were whitecaps on the puddles. Suddenly the night sky was split by a fork of lightning. Thunder boomed close by. I shivered.

    – *Reminds me of home*, said Norbert with a sigh.

"The rain?"

    – *No, the thunder. On Jupiter it thunders all the time.*

"Tell me more about Jupiter," I said. "Do you miss it?"

    – *Oh yes.* He was silent for a moment. I wondered what it would be like to be four hundred million miles away from home.

    – *Mostly what I think about are the smells of home. Smells are what you remember best. On Jupiter there are flowers everywhere, and shops selling cheeses. Ahh!"*

I didn't know how I felt about cheeses. "You know what I've always liked?" I said. "I've always liked the smell of chlorine. Swimming pools smell like that."

    – *Oh yes. Chlorine is great. And wood burning in a fireplace. Apple wood is nice.*

Norbert was right. Smells are very strong in your memory. "Is that why you decided to stay in my nose?" I asked. "To be close to the smells?"

    – *I'm here because I fit here. And it's a great space for me.*

Jupiter is a big planet but it's crowded. Here I don't usually have to worry about intrusions. Hey!

I hastily removed my finger. I hadn't even realized what I was doing. "Sorry."

– *What else do you like the smell of?* he asked.

I had my eyes closed, remembering. "Oranges at Christmas," I said. "And grass early on a summer morning."

– *What about bacon?*

"Yes, bacon's not bad. Sort of sweet and smoky at the same time." We hadn't had bacon for awhile. We used to have it more often when Dad was around. Mom says it makes a big mess and doesn't give you much nutrition. "Bacon-flavored potato chips are good too."

– *Or sour cream and onion. Mmmmm.*

We've had this discussion several times. "What about that old book I opened at the library?" I said. "Remember – the big old atlas with the funny pictures in the maps? I liked the spicy dusty smell. It was like the smell of secrets."

– *Or the fall fairground. Remember? Straw and candy and grease and lots of people? That was the smell of excitement.*

"Or the first warm day of the year, after months and months of winter. It's the day you take off your big coat for the first time, and feel the sun on your back. It's all the growing things peeping through the cold wet earth . . . it's like the smell of hope."

– *Warm bread fresh from the oven.*

"Bedsheets that have been dried outside on the clothesline."

73

— Or the smell of your mom, when she bends over to kiss you goodnight. Her hair and maybe her face powder, and the smell of her cheek against yours.

The smell of love. I nodded without saying anything.

Norbert liked talking about Jupiter, but it made him homesick. "Why don't you go home then?" I asked him. He said he would, one day. He was going to regret leaving the space in my nose, he said, but he missed his parents. I talked about my parents too: told him how screwed up they were, how bad I felt that they weren't together. And that they didn't really love me. Especially Dad.

What is it about dads? They're the ones who leave, so what does it matter if they love you? You never saw them when they lived at home, and you never see them after they go. I don't know, but it would make all the difference in the world if my dad would say he loves me. Just once. If your folks are separated, you'll know what I mean.

Mom is different. She loves everybody. Maybe it would be nice to hear her say she loves me more than anyone else . . . more than her work, anyway. But I don't *worry* about her love. Maybe because she's there day after day telling me to tidy my room. Maybe because moms are, well, moms. But my dad . . . would it hurt him to give me a hug? One hug? To tell me he loves me? Oh well.

It was a really nasty storm. The sky opened up like a cardboard carton and poured rain all over everything. The wind rattled the windows and moaned around the chimney.

"Listen to that weather," my mom said, tucking me into bed. "Sounds like winter's coming pretty soon."

"I'm glad I'm inside," I told her. She kissed me and closed the door on her way out.

– *No night for nose or beast*, said Norbert.

Mom poked her head back in. "Did you say something?"

"Just goodnight," I said.

"Night."

9

WAY TO GO, SQUEAKY!

The next day was bright and still, and the ground was covered in frost. My feet sounded like I was walking on tiny fragments of broken glass as I made my way down our street to Victor's. His mom opened the door.

"Hello there, you darling boy," she said with a bigger-than-usual smile for me. "Victor's already gone to school," she said. "He took a lift with his father this morning."

"Oh." I wondered what was going on. Victor hated driving with his dad in the grocery van. Usually he waited for me. "I'll be going then," I said.

"I hope you enjoy your assembly this afternoon. I hear she's really something. I'm that tempted to go myself."

I wondered who Mrs. Grunewald was talking about. I waved good-bye and left.

I walked the long way to school again, arriving with not much time to spare. The playground was a hive of gossip. Groups of kids and teachers buzzed at each other, broke off, and reformed in different groups.

"I hope she sings 'Don't Be Stupid.'"

"I hear she's going to try out something new."

"What'll she wear?"

". . . been going through old yearbooks and I can't find her."

"Maybe it's not her real name."

Who were they talking about? I went up to the nearest group and asked what was going on. "Haven't you heard?" they said. "Don't you know about the special guest at our assembly?"

"Someone who used to go to school here," I said. "I didn't hear who."

"Well, it's –"

The lineup bell rang, and my informant ran away without telling me.

I found Victor in line. "What happened to you this morning?" I asked. "I went by your place and your mom said you'd already left."

"Sorry, Alan. It's just that . . . I was worried. You know the Cougars have sworn to get you for making all those comments during the game yesterday."

"Oh."

"Why did you do it, Alan? You made them so mad. Prudence especially. You know her . . . she's going to kill you. And I . . . I didn't want her to think . . ."

"That you were a friend of mine? In case she kills you too?"

"Well . . . yes."

"Oh," I said.

"Just until she beats you up. Then I'll walk to school with you again."

"Thanks a lot, Vic."

"Unless you can't walk. Then you and I can both get a lift with my father. In the van."

I nodded. "Thanks. And smell like onions?"

His face fell. He looked up and down the line, and then surreptitiously sniffed his hands and under his arms. "Is that what I smell like? Honest?"

Poor Victor. "I was just kidding," I said.

"No, really, don't kid me about this. Do I smell like onions?"

A teacher told us to find our places in line. I left Victor sniffing and asking the guy behind him if he smelled onions.

"Hi," said Miranda. I said "Hi" back, and slipped in behind her.

"Going to be a great assembly," she said. "I'm so glad we won the intramural trophy. She's going to present it to us . . . and shake our hands. Isn't that great?"

"Who?" I asked. "Who are we all talking about?"

The bell rang again. Time to go in. We started to shuffle

78

forward. Miranda was still favoring her ankle, I noticed. She whispered over her shoulder. "Shania Twain! Isn't that great!"

– *Great! Just great!* said Norbert.

"You sound enthusiastic, Squeaky. I'm glad you're a country music fan." She smiled at me.

"There's a part of me that really likes it," I said. "Something inside me."

"I didn't know that. You're just full of surprises, aren't you?"

I didn't say anything.

"Anyway, I thought Shania was from Timmins. I never knew she used to go to school here."

The morning passed uneventfully, except for this ripple of country music excitement that wouldn't die down. Norbert was as bad as anyone else. I tried telling him that Shania Twain was not coming, but he wouldn't believe it. And every time he heard someone else talk about her, he got more and more convinced. The principal didn't make matters better by reminding us about the assembly during morning announcements. "It'll be a great show," said Mr. Omerod. "I hope you're all looking forward to meeting a truly remarkable individual."

We were doing *flora* in science class – that's plants. Animals are *fauna*. Pretty dull, whatever you call it. Even Miss Scathely looked bored. She was going around the class asking us to think of different kinds of trees. "Do you have a tree in your backyard?" she'd ask. There was a growing list of trees on the board. I don't know what I was thinking of when she asked me. My mind went blank. I couldn't think of a single kind of tree. Not one. I looked up at the board for guidance, and one entry caught my eye: slippery elm. That's the tree in the school yard, the one the bullies hung around before school. I pictured Prudence – braided hair, unsmiling face, matching sweater and slacks, heavy shoes. Perfect for kicking, I thought.

"Alan?" prompted Miss Scathely. "Are you paying attention?"

All around me was a kind of bored silence – no one cared whether I was paying attention or not – and then, with nothing useful going on in my head, Norbert spoke up.

– *What about shoe-trees?* he asked.

The class stirred slightly. Miss Scathely smiled. "I don't think those are the kind of trees we're talking about, er, Alan," she said.

– *They're the kind of trees we have on Jupiter*, said Norbert.

"I beg your pardon?"

– *Ah, the trees of Jupiter! The richly scented umbrella-trees, the deep and musty shoe-trees, the high roof-trees, the hard-working axle-trees, the sweet and tender pace-trees! And in every household, blooming and blossoming, a completely unique family-tree. Sometimes I wish I'd never left.* He sighed.

Now the class was awake. Most of them were giggling. I blushed Dingwall red, but I didn't move. Actually, it was kind of nice to be able to make people laugh. Without even opening my mouth too.

"What are pace-trees?" Miss Scathely asked.

– *They're beautiful! Tarts and éclairs and layer cakes. Mmm! The scent of them on the summer breeze.*

"You mean pastries," she said, laughing.

– *Didn't I say that?*

Miss Scathely didn't say anything about Norbert's voice. She didn't seem to notice at all. She leaned back against her desk. "Isn't that interesting. I can just imagine what shoe-trees and pace-trees would look like, if they really were flora. Let's turn this into a game. Can anyone think of any other kind of tree they might have on Jupiter?"

After a moment Miranda put up her hand. "What about industry?" she asked. Miss Scathely nodded her approval.

"Yes, I can just imagine a crop of heavy indus-trees being cut down for timber." The class laughed appreciatively. "Anyone else now? Wait – I've got one." She went to the board and drew a sharp, angular outline of a tree. The foliage at the top looked like a triangle. "All right, class, what kind of tree is this?"

Three or four voices came together. "It's a geomet-tree!"

Miss Scathely grinned.

She drew another tree – this one had cans and jars and boxes hanging from the branches. No one said anything. She added a dangling skillet. I was trying to work it out but couldn't.

– It is! It's a pan-tree! Norbert sounded wistful.

"Good," said Miss Scathely.

I couldn't help wondering if there were any lava-trees, and what their leaves would look like.

– That's exactly what a real pan-tree looks like. I can't remember the last time I saw one. The ones on Jupiter are so lovely, full of gold and silver flowers. They're not at all like the carpen-trees, with their sharp needles and spikes.

The class laughed and laughed. Miranda started clapping, and the other kids joined in. "Way to go, Squeaky," somebody shouted from the back of the room.

"Who's Squeaky?" Miss Scathely asked. And everyone except me – everyone including Norbert – shouted my name.

"Well, Squeaky, you make Jupiter sound like an interesting place," Miss Scathely told me.

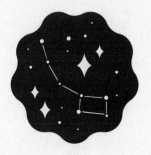

10

NOT A PRINCIPAL
KIND OF JOKE

Our principal, Mr. Omerod, stood at the microphone, smiling hard. "I'd like all of you to give a warm Edgewood Senior Public School welcome to Captain Sid Allinson," he said.

The tall stranger onstage, the guy we'd been trying to identify, stood up. He was square-shouldered, with a clean face and short hair. He had on a blue uniform with red doodads on the shoulders. He ducked his head modestly. The principal held up his hands and clapped them together.

Poor Captain Allinson. A huge and spontaneous roar of applause did not raise the roof of the auditorium. No one fainted. No one rushed onstage. No one whistled. Instead, the entire auditorium dissolved in a sea of tossed and disjointed murmurs. "Who's he?" "What's he done?" And then three hundred people turned to their neighbors and whispered, "Where's Shania Twain?" From where I was sitting, off to the side of the darkened auditorium, waiting to go onstage later to receive my intramural ribbon, it sounded like a disappointed giant sucking up the end of a milkshake. The principal went on.

"I remember Sid in 1979, back when I taught physical education. He was a keen high jumper, but I hardly knew back then that he would end up in outer space. That's a pretty impressive high jump . . . even with a rocket assist."

Mr. Omerod smiled. This was a principal kind of joke. Captain Sid recognized it, and laughed politely. The rest of the audience was still too disappointed to respond.

"No doubt you have been following Sid's exploits in the newspapers," he said. "As the third Canadian in space, he has represented our country with honor and dignity. His mission with NASA was an unqualified success. The space shuttle Columbia successfully repaired a malfunctioning satellite. Sid, and the rest of the crew, met with the . . . was it the vice president?" He looked over. Sid nodded. "The vice president of the United States. Sid also met with the prime minister in Ottawa, and now he's back home, using his fame and his knowledge to teach schoolchildren about space and science. A wonderful role model for the youth of today. And to think he was once a student in this very audi-torium. He sat where you are sitting today. It's enough to make you consider what you plan to do with your own life. Someday you may be sitting where he is now."

Silence. And then, from the shielding darkness at the

back of the auditorium, a plaintive question drifted out into the air. "But can he sing?"

No one dared to laugh.

The principal frowned. Captain Sid approached the microphone clutching a sheaf of notes. He was a little nervous. The lukewarm reception wasn't helping any. He probably felt he was better off in outer space. I'll bet a lot of people would rather be in outer space than in front of a microphone at a middle-school assembly.

I don't know if Sid, as he asked us all to call him, ever understood what was going on. Rumors spread like weeds, and somehow in less than a day the entire school – from little Marianne Macadam, who could walk into a locker without turning sideways, to Mr. Valentine, guidance counselor and noted fan of country music – expected to see Shania Twain onstage.

The captain got off to a bad start. "Hi there, boys and girls," he said.

Don't you hate it when they do that? There should be a handbook for guest speakers at assemblies. Never call boys and girls "boys and girls." Don't call us "kids" either. Don't refer to status at all. The correct greeting at an assembly is, "Hi." Unless you're famous. Then you say, "Hi, I'm Shania Twain."

"I'm, uh, a captain," he said, pointing to his uniform, "but I've never been on a boat." He stopped again. The principal laughed – it was his sort of joke. The rest of us didn't. The captain peered at his notes.

"Now, boys and girls, I want to show you some really interesting pictures I took on my last trip." Behind him, the curtains parted to reveal the big white viewing screen. Last month a public health nurse had shown us pictures of blackened and decaying lungs on that very screen.

We sighed and settled back in our chairs. Disappointment was giving way to resignation. At least we knew where we were now. This was going to be another slide show . . . which, all things considered, was still better than environmental studies class.

Victor was beside me. I guess he didn't mind sitting near me in the dark. I whispered, "You know, your dad would have been better than this guy. He might have brought some free samples."

Then the spotlight went out and a big star map came on.

Norbert woke up about halfway through the assembly. He takes afternoon naps – that's the part of him that's still only three years old. Sometimes a whole afternoon will pass without a squeak out of him. Anyway, it wasn't until we were listening to Captain Sid tell us about constellations that I felt a familiar prickling in my nose.

– *What's going on?* Norbert whispered – not really a whisper, more a buzzing sound. Victor, and Miranda, who was sitting on the other side of me, were probably the only people besides me who heard it.

– *You promised you'd wake me when the assembly started!*

"Sh," I whispered.

– *Hey!* I could feel my nostrils flaring. Norbert must have been really excited.

– *That's not Shania Twain,* he said, more audibly.

Oh no. "Quiet, Norbert," I whispered. I bent forward in my seat.

"Are you all right?" Miranda asked. She and Victor exchanged looks behind my back.

– *Is Shania Twain on later?*

"Yes," I whispered. "Later." Later tonight, on television. "Now be quiet and listen."

Everyone in the auditorium was half asleep by now. Even the principal, whose silhouette was visible in the wash of light between slides, had covered a couple of yawns. Captain Allinson, however great an astronaut and role model he was, was not a gripping public speaker.

"The constellations represent a very small portion of the stars you can see at night. You see, constellations are all made of fixed stars. They don't change from year to year or from century to century. Most stars are not fixed, though. They are, uh, how can I put it –"

– *Broken?* Norbert interrupted in a loud voice.

There was a titter from the audience, and Captain Allinson gave a wary smile. "In motion," he said. The captain was using a light pointer to show us bits of the slide that he was talking about. "These stars," he said as he moved the pointer over the center of the slide, "form the constellation which the ancient Greeks named after the great hunter, Orion. These three stars in a row here are supposed to represent his, uh, belt."

– You're wrong! said Norbert, pretty loudly.

Of course, he's an experienced space traveler. The principal sat up. Everyone sat up.

– Look at it! Does it look like a hunter? Does it?

"You'd better be quiet, Squeaky," Miranda whispered.

"I can't help it," I whispered back. "It's Norbert talking, not me."

The Captain was peering out but he couldn't see me in the darkness. He was pretty good about being interrupted. "The Greeks had wonderfully good imaginations," he said.

– They had wonderfully bad eyesight.

Lots of people could hear Norbert now. There were some snickers. A couple of teachers were calling "Sh!"

"I'd better get out of here," I whispered.

"Do you need help?" Miranda sounded concerned.

"Better leave him alone," said Victor.

I ducked down out of my seat and started to edge my way along the row. "Excuse me," I murmured to my classmates. With luck I could make it to the door.

Norbert was still talking.

– And that idea of astrogation guidance is very primitive. On my spaceship . . .

Captain Allinson changed the slide. I was almost at the end of the row.

"Here," he said, "we have a familiar constellation."

– The Cocoa Jug! I was covering Norbert with my hand, but enough people heard him to start a pretty good chuckle

going through the audience. I swear I heard someone whisper, "Squeaky." Sure sounded like it. The principal walked to the edge of the stage.

"Who is that?" he asked angrily. I was crouched down, and it was too dark for him to see clearly, but he was staring right in my direction.

"Ursa Minor," the captain said. "The Little Bear. It does look a bit like a jug, doesn't it?"

– *Hey, where are we going?* I was crawling on my hands and knees now, racing up the aisle to the rear doors. "Shut up!" I panted.

– *I don't want to miss the country music.* And then I was pushing the auditorium door open. Light streamed into the darkened room.

The principal called out, "There he goes! Stop him, someone!" but by then I was running down the hall holding my nose. I decided to head for the nearest washroom. I passed a janitor on the way, who asked if I was all right.

"Nosebleed," I told him, over my shoulder.

I can't stare down at my nose without crossing my eyes – a mirror is helpful. So I stood in front of the mirror in the downstairs BOYS bathroom and stared at Norbert.

"I hope you're pleased," I said. "Do you know how much trouble we're in?"

He didn't reply. My nose was wrinkled up, the way it is when I'm embarrassed, or when the air smells bad. The stall doors were all closed. I noticed them over my shoulder.

"The Cocoa Jug," I said bitterly. Norbert didn't reply.

Was that a wisp of smoke rising from behind the closed door of the nearest stall? I stared harder. Yes it was. The room smelled of smoke too. No wonder my nose was all wrinkled up. Someone was smoking a cigarette in a stall in the BOYS bathroom.

No, not someone. More than one person. There were two wisps of smoke. Three wisps. All the stalls were occupied, but . . . by whom? Who would be smoking cigarettes when they should be at the assembly? I'd noticed Mary in the auditorium.

I raced to the bathroom door, but stopped when I heard voices in the hall outside.

"He ran this way," said the janitor. "Said he had a nose-bleed. I can't tell exactly what he sounded like . . . he talked kind of funny."

Oh oh.

I ran back to the sink in time to hear the hiss of a cigarette butt dropped into a toilet bowl. And another. And an "Ouch!" Gary's voice; he must have burnt himself. The toilets flushed together. I ran back to the door. The voices outside were getting closer. I returned to the mirror; my heart doing handstands in my chest. I felt like a trapped rat. Do you know how many good hiding places there are in a school bathroom, not counting the stalls? That's right. None. The next moment the stall doors opened and Gary, Larry, and Prudence stepped out. They were smiling, even Prudence, who never smiles.

"Do you know," she asked, "how much trouble *you're* in?"

11

GETTING AWAY WITH IT

You think about the stupidest things. "What are you doing in the BOYS bathroom?" I asked Prudence. It was another reason to be impressed by her. I'd be way too embarrassed to even go into the GIRLS bathroom, let alone sit in a stall and have a smoke.

She didn't answer. I backed away from her, toward the door. I planned to run as fast as I could out into the hall and throw myself on Principal Omerod's mercy. When worst comes to worst, pick the lesser of two evils, and a lecture was a lot less painful than being killed. Not even Patrick Henry would have picked death before detention.

I turned around, but Prudence didn't give me a chance to get to the door. Her hand flashed out. Faster than a striking snake, she grabbed me by the collar of my shirt, and pulled me backward. I choked as the front of my shirt collar bit into my neck. Prudence kept pulling until I collapsed and fell to the floor. Cold floors in public bathrooms . . . you ever noticed? Maybe not . . . maybe you've never lain down on one. I stared up at Prudence's face. And Gary's and Larry's. I tried to shout, but all that came out was a weak little rattling sound. I tried to prepare myself for pain . . . which is impossible. No matter how hard you prepare yourself, the pain is a surprise. It hurts. I can remember every needle I ever got. I can remember every time I pulled off a bandaid, or watched my mom dig out a splinter. I always tried to prepare myself for the pain . . . and it never worked.

First Gary kicked me. They say you're not supposed to kick someone when he's down, but Gary's a real bully, and that's what bullies do. He kicked me in the rear end, and I'd like to say that he hurt his foot, but he didn't. "Ouch," I tried to say. Not much of a sound came out. Then he made a mistake. He bent over and, as a way of making fun of me, he tweaked Norbert.

Big mistake.

– *Oooh!* A surprisingly intense high-pitched shriek. Gary straightened up. And so, somehow, some incredible how, did I. It felt like I'd been given a jolt of electricity. One moment I was on my back, looking up at my tormentors, unable even to utter . . . and the next moment I was on my feet, heart racing, muscles tensed, ready for action, with a martial arts battle cry raising the roof off the bathroom.

Of course, it wasn't my war cry. It was Norbert's.

– *Hee-Yup!* he shouted. *Attack! Attack! Attack! It is death!*
He sounded like a samurai chipmunk. Gary backed away
with a strange look on his face. He probably thought I was
crazy – and I'm not saying it was an unreasonable thought.
He put his hands out to protect himself if I started punching, but I didn't start punching. I didn't lift my hands. I
rushed right at him, jumped in the air, and smashed him
in the face with my . . . well, it's hard to say what part of
me I smashed him with. Norbert led the way, but I suspect
he ducked at the last minute, and let my forehead do the
actual work. It all happened pretty quickly.

Whatever it was, it worked a treat. I didn't feel a thing, and
there was Gary screaming and crying out and holding his
nose. Blood dripped through his fingers like grape drink
from a leaky juice box – that happened to me last week and
it got over everything in my lunch.

For just a second Prudence and Larry were too shocked
to act . . . and in that second, I made my move. I took a
step forward, slipped, and fell to the floor. Not my best
move. Both of them leaped to block my exit. Larry gave
this big, dumb, surprised laugh. They had me now, and we
all knew it. A curious sense of acceptance settled on me
like a blanket. I wasn't going to struggle anymore.

Nice friends they were. They didn't care about Gary at all.
He was slumped against the sink, fumbling for a paper towel
to stanch the blood. Neither of them spared him a glance.

"You're dead, Dingwall," whispered Prudence.

"Okay," I said.

"We're going to beat the stuffing out of you," she said.

"Okay."

"You called us all names on the soccer field. You humiliated us. We can't let you get away with that. You just smashed Gary's nose. We can't let you get away with that either. Do you understand?"

"Okay."

I don't know what was going on with me. It was like I was under a spell. I might as well have been one of those dolls that says the same thing over and over again. Pull my string and I say, "Okay."

"You're going to whine and beg for mercy, but you won't get it. You'll never call anyone names ever again. Is that . . . okay?"

"That's just fine," I said.

"Ready, Larry? On the count of three. One, two –" and then the principal came into the bathroom, and the whole situation changed immediately.

"What's going on here?" asked Mr. Omerod in a very principal kind of voice.

Behind him, in a different kind of voice, the janitor said, "Hey!" – meaning the same thing.

There was so much for them to look at – blood and paper towels, a girl in the boys' room – that they didn't notice me right away. I saw a way of avoiding both death and detention. I scuttled into the nearest stall, crouched on the toilet seat, and shut the door quietly while the bullies still blocked me from view. I didn't want the janitor remembering my yellow shirt.

"Prudence, why are you in the boys' room? Why weren't you other two at the assembly?" asked the principal.

Silence, except for Gary whimpering. Poor Gary, the principal didn't seem to care about his wound either. I shut my mouth and hoped no one would notice the noise my heart made, beating inside my chest. To me, it sounded like Paul Bunyan splitting logs.

"I slipped out of the assembly to go to the bathroom," Prudence explained. "On my way back to the auditorium I passed the boys' room and heard Gary crying out for help. Of course I went in. Gary was standing at the sink, like that, with a bloody nose. Larry was already helping him. Then you came in. Sir," she added.

A fast thinker, Prudence. I wondered if Mr. Omerod would believe her story. He sniffed the air, which still reeked of cigarette smoke. "What about you two?" he asked.

"Oh, uh. It was just like she said," said Larry. He wasn't a fast thinker. "I was helping Gary here, and she came in."

Gary whimpered quietly.

"Hmm. So this is the boy you saw in the hall, Mr. Keenan."

"Well, sir." The janitor didn't sound sure of himself. Gary is taller and darker-haired than I am, and his face doesn't look anything like mine. But the janitor only saw me for a second, and never saw my face. "I guess it could have been," he said. "He does have a nosebleed."

"Were you interrupting our special guest at the assembly, Gary?" asked the principal.

"No, sir," Gary whimpered.

"Were you, Prudence?"

"No."

"How about you, Larry?"

"Huh? No, sir. Course not." Larry was able to answer honestly. He hadn't been interrupting the assembly . . . he hadn't even been at the assembly.

The principal sighed. "Very well. Gary, your bleeding seems to have stopped. Report to the nurse's office. I will send someone to see you in a few minutes. Prudence and Larry, go back to the auditorium for the last part of the program."

"Yes, sir." I could hear the relief in Larry's voice. They were going to get away with it. He was tempted to improvise. "Great show, isn't it, sir?"

"What do you mean?"

"Shania Twain, sir. She's giving us a great show. We don't usually listen to her music – Prudence and Gary and me – but we agreed that seeing her live, like this, was . . . really. . . ."

His voice trailed away. He had broken the first rule of Getting Away With It, the rule kids are supposed to learn early in life. Never say more than you have to. No one ever got spanked for saying too little.

Mr. Omerod was decisive. "All three of you . . . detention for missing the assembly. Report to my office immediately after school. Now march back to the auditorium with me."

As their footsteps faded away, I heard Larry say, "Ouch!" I wondered which of the other two had kicked him.

Miranda and I talked for a bit while we were waiting for the school bus to come and carry her home. I got a few looks from the other bus kids. Admiring looks. I wasn't used to being noticed, but I didn't mind. When I told Miranda about the bathroom episode, she laughed. "That was very brave of you," she said. "But those Cougars are so awful. It sounds like they really mean to get you. It'll probably blow over in a week or so, but I don't like to think of you in danger, Alan."

"Me neither," I said. I didn't think it would blow over so soon, but I didn't want to whine.

The bus pulled up then. Miranda hoisted her knapsack on her shoulder and gave my . . . well, gave Norbert, an affectionate tweak. "The Cocoa Jug," she said, shaking her head.

It wasn't a bad afternoon for November, a bit windy but lots of sun and not too cool. I had my coat unzipped and my hands in my pockets. I could hear a cardinal singing high up in a tree nearby. I was worried about the bullies, but I was happy too. I was happier than I was worried, but I didn't know why.

– *You're cheerful enough*, Norbert commented.

"Aren't you?"

– *I don't know. I'm kind of . . . homesick.* He sighed.

"For Jupiter?"

– *Maybe it was seeing the Cocoa Jug, so clear and bright. I used to look out of my window and see it. Every night. My mom used to tell me how once, long ago, the cocoa spilled out of the jug, along with all the little marshmallows, and together they make up the band of light crossing the sky at night. I can't remember what you call it . . . not "Mars," but something like that.*

"Milky Way?" I suggested.

– *Yes, that's it. I knew it was some kind of chocolate bar.* He sighed again.

I was at the King Street bridge now. I stopped to look over the side. The river ran full and brown underneath me. I couldn't see any fish. I never can, except in summer when the water is slack and low, and the big lazy carp come up from the lake and hang about, eating garbage – at least that's what Victor says. For sure they don't eat the worms we try to catch them with.

I unlocked the front door of the house and let myself in. The place was empty, as usual. Mom wouldn't be back from work for an hour or more. There were two phone messages. I got myself some milk and cookies while I listened to them. The first message was a kid calling for Mom. He didn't sound much older than I am. He was being accused of something he didn't do. "Oh, you poor thing," I mumbled through a mouthful of chocolate chip.

The second message was for me. I hadn't heard my dad's voice for awhile, and it took me a moment to recognize it. "Sorry, son," his recorded voice said. "I won't be able to fly in to see you this weekend. I know we were planning to make a day of it, go to a movie and then maybe take in a game at the Gardens. I was looking forward to it. But I have to talk to this important guy from Hong Kong, and he's only in Vancouver for a couple of days. Sorry I missed you. I'll try and call again later on. Bye."

And then the house was filled up with a big deep echoing silence, and I went downstairs to the TV room. My good mood wasn't as good anymore. I was feeling homesick too, just like Norbert. Only I was already home. I was homesick for a home I didn't have anymore.

I watched TV until Mom came home and started clattering pots and pans in the kitchen. She seemed to make more noise than she needed, as if she were angry and didn't know any other way to show it. Or else she didn't like the silence any more than I did.

12

THEY REALLY LIKE ME

Dinner was chicken tenders. That's what they call them; I
don't think either part of the name is right. They came out
of the freezer with the succotash. There was steamed rice
too. Mom likes rice, and I don't, so we tend to have rice
more often when she's mad at me, and less often when she's
happy. The rice-o-meter is a sure sign of my standing. Last
summer when I broke the aerial off her car playing football, we had rice seven days in a row.

We ate in silence, except for the rustling of pages. I
was reading a book about a lost bat who was searching
for the rest of his colony, and Mom was reading a case
file. Every now and then she asked me questions: "How
was school?" "Did you finish your homework?" "Do you
want some more succotash?" And I said, "Fine," "Just

about," and "No." Succotash – now that's something that tastes like its name.

After dinner I went to Victor's house, ostensibly because we are working on a science project together, but really because I wanted to play *NHL Hockey* on his computer. The project isn't due until the end of term. Lots of time for that. But the hockey game, and the joystick you need to play it, were brand new.

His mom opened the door with a big smile. "Come on in, Alan," she said. "We're just sitting down to dinner. Of course you'll join us."

"I've already had –"

She didn't let me finish. "Just a bite then," she said. Victor's mom put her arm around me on the way in to the kitchen. She always seems to be on her way to the kitchen. It's the air she likes to breathe . . . if she's away for too long, she starts to gasp.

"Are you having chicken tenders?" I asked.

She frowned. "What are they?"

"I don't know," I said. "But we get them all the time."

There was a huge pot of stew on the stove, with sausage and potatoes and chunky, pale-colored vegetables. At home I hadn't wanted anything more to eat, but I found enough room inside me for a whole plateful. "What's this vegetable?" I asked. "It's not cabbage."

"No." Her eyes sparkled. "Do you not like cabbage, Alan? Last time you couldn't really decide whether you liked it or not."

Norbert liked it. I hated it. But I didn't tell Mrs. Grunewald that. "I like this," I said.

Victor and his dad shared a smile. They were both hearty eaters.

"It's turnip," his mom said.

I frowned. I hate turnip. Or I thought I did.

A small kitchen radio was playing classical music in the background. Very busy stuff, and familiar too – I couldn't help smiling. Mr. Grunewald was listening. I could tell because he chewed along with it. When the music speeded up, so did his chewing. "That's beautiful," he said, finishing a bite. I wondered if he was referring to the food or the music. When we listen to the radio at dinnertime, it's generally a news show. Hard to get excited at how beautiful the news is.

The Grunewald family talked about all sorts of weird things. Victor's parents kept wanting to know how he *felt*. Did he really like Miss Scathely? Was he worried about the math test? They asked me too: How did I feel about boys wearing earrings? That boy with all the earrings, that Gary – a no-good boy, didn't I think so?

I stared. Mom and I didn't talk like this. It was almost embarrassing. "A no-good boy," I told Mrs. Grunewald. "But not because of the earrings."

"No no, put the chicken before the egg." That was Mr. Grunewald. "A good kind of boy wouldn't get his ears pierced in the first place."

The music ended. An announcer's voice came on. Mr. Grunewald held out his plate for another helping of stew.

"Do you like this music, Alan?" he asked. "A great composer, Rossini, don't you think?"

"I've heard his stuff on 'Bugs Bunny,'" I said. Victor snickered. I don't know what he thought was so funny. That's why the music was familiar. I could picture Daffy Duck running away from Elmer Fudd.

Mr. Grunewald frowned and said something that sounded like, "Hmph."

A gold intramural award ribbon was pinned to the bulletin board. Grade Seven Champions, it said. The only things we pin up in our kitchen are school announcements and 50%-off coupons. There's a drawer in my desk where I keep personal stuff – a picture of me and my dad holding up fish we'd caught, a copy of the local newspaper from last year, when it printed a story of mine.

Dessert was messy; a flaky pastry with fruit inside it, and white sugar dust on top. I must have thanked Mrs. Grunewald a dozen times. Victor and his dad smiled and smiled.

"Now boys, off you go," said Mrs. Grunewald, shooing us out of the kitchen. "I know you want to work on your project. No, John!" She slapped Mr. Grunewald on the arm. He was trying to cut himself another piece of dessert.

In his room Victor breathed a sigh of relief. "Sorry," he said. "My mom is a bit . . ."

"That's okay," I said. "I like your mom. And the food was good. Even the turnip."

"Yeah, she's a good cook. If only she didn't . . . care so much!"

It seemed like an odd thing to say. He made it sound like a burden.

The computer was already on. He took two CDs from a dustproof rack. *World Encyclopedia* and *NHL*. "You want hockey first?" he said, "Or science?"

Dumb question. "He shoots! He scores!" I said.

"You sure? What about: He researches! He organizes data!"

"Vic –"

"He observes! He draws conclusions!"

I punched him in the arm.

"Okay, okay." He loaded the CD into the drive.

We played for an hour or so. He won almost every game, but I had fun, and we did manage to do a bit of work on our project before I had to go home.

Both of Victor's parents came to the door to see me off. I thanked Mrs. Grunewald again for supper. She beamed and said to come back soon.

"You don't know anything about music," said Mr. Grunewald, slapping me on the back. "But you're a good boy."

Tell me, why did that statement make me want to cry on the walk home?

– *Hey! It's leaking in here. What's the matter?*

"I don't know."

– *You're not getting a cold are you? You know how I hate it when you catch a cold.*

"I'm just a little upset," I said. "My dad never tells me I'm a good boy."

– *Oh. Well look, if I tell you you're a good boy, will you stop dripping? The carpet in the back room is soaked.*

Norbert is so sympathetic.

– *I'm wearing rubber boots in here.*

I couldn't help myself. I had to smile.

There aren't any streetlamps around the bend from Victor's house to mine. Night covered me like a blanket. The full moon looked close enough to touch.

"I wish I didn't have to go home to my mom, sometimes," I said.

Norbert sighed. – *That's funny. Sometimes I wish I could.*

"Did you and Victor have fun?" my mom called from the kitchen.

"Uh huh," I said.

"A girl telephoned a few minutes ago. Miranda, she said her name was. I took down her number."

I hung up my coat and went into the kitchen. Mom sat at a corner of the table; a stack of files balanced precariously nearby. I had this insane urge to topple them all over.

"You know, Mom, the Grunewalds like me. They really like me."

She looked up, briefly, smiling with her mouth but not her eyes. "That's nice, dear."

13

WHAT RHYMES
WITH MIRANDA?

I'd never phoned Miranda before. I was surprised to find that my fingers were slippery as I punched the number. I was breathing fast too.

Our phone is in the kitchen. Not very private, with my mom working just a few feet away. I keep asking Mom for a phone in my bedroom, and she keeps saying, "One of these days." I wonder which one she means. Miranda's line was busy. I ran upstairs, sweating gently.

– *What is going on?* Norbert sounded peeved.

"Nothing," I said.

– *It's suddenly very hot in here, and I can hear your heart thudding away like a bass drum. Are you sick or something?*

"I don't think so."

I sat down and tried to do some homework, but I wasn't paying attention. Norbert interrupted me. – *It's her, isn't it? You're thinking about her.*

"Who?" I blustered. "I don't know who you're talking about."

– *Look at your homework, Mr. Convincing.*

I looked down, and there was Miranda's name, all over my spelling workbook.

Oh. "Well, yes, I guess I am, a bit," I said.

– *Hey, that's okay. I've been in love myself. Her name was Nerissa, and I still miss her – hey, that almost rhymes. I wonder what she's doing now?*

"I'm not in love!" I said.

– *Eh? Oh no, of course not.*

"I'm not, I tell you."

– *Uh huh.*

We both knew I was lying. I took out a fresh sheet of paper, and thoughtfully wrote down the name again. Miranda. "Say, Norbert, you've given me an idea. You know a lot of words," I said. "Can you think of anything that rhymes with Miranda?"

– *Going to write a poem?* he asked.

"Maybe," I admitted.

He thought for a moment.

– *Verandah*, he said.

"Like porch? That kind of verandah?" Not exactly a romantic inspiration. My mom and dad had rented a cottage with a verandah a few years ago. I'd been sitting on the verandah when a giant spider dropped from the ceiling. Plop – right into my lap! Thing was the size of my fist. Scared the curds and whey right out of me.

– *Hey, don't blame me . . . talk to her parents. They could have named her Jane or Sue.*

"I don't see what I can do with verandah," I said.

– *How about* –

Miranda, Miranda, I pace the verandah,
Remembering all about you.
Your eyes that gleam, your jaws that expand-ah
While on your sandwich you chew.

"I don't know," I said.

– *I think you're the greatest, no libel or sland-ah*
Could take anything from your charms.
My heartstrings stretch like a big rubber band-ah
When I hold you close in my –

"Alan?" My mom knocked at the door. "Is everything all right?"

"Fine," I said. "Just fine, Mom. Goodnight." She goes to bed before I do, because she has to be out of the house so early.

"Goodnight." She hesitated outside the door for a moment, then sighed and walked away. A minute later the phone rang.

"Hi," I said.

"Alan, is that you? You sound all out of breath."

"Oh hi, Miranda," I said. Norbert snorted. I held the phone away from my mouth and tried to relax. "I, uh, tried to call you earlier," I said. "But your line was busy."

"Oh. Sorry."

"That's okay."

Silence.

"I'm, uh, glad you phoned," I said.

"That's nice."

More silence.

– *Gee, this is like Romeo and Juliet,* said Norbert.

"Shut up!" I whispered.

– *So much poetry! So much romance! Come on, Miranda, can't you tell that I'm crazy about you!*

I drew in my breath sharply. I could feel myself blushing . . . I wondered if Miranda could feel me blushing through the phone wire. That's how hot I felt.

"Why, Squeaky!" she said, sounding kind of hot and bothered herself. "I'm so glad you told me," she said. "I was beginning to worry; you see, I feel kind of like that about you."

"You do?" I shrieked – or maybe it was Norbert. Maybe we both shouted together. And . . . well, I'm not going to go into too much detail over the next five minutes or so. At the end of it, Norbert said, – *Whew! Now that's more like it!*

Miranda laughed. "There is something I want to ask you, though, Alan. I was just thinking now . . . well, I mean, I always sort of liked you. Even last year. And now that I know you better, how funny you are and everything, I like you even more. But . . . well, what I'm saying, is . . . oh, this is going to sound stupid."

"No no, go on," I said.

"Well . . . there isn't *really* anyone living in your nose, is there?"

I didn't know what to say. "Well," I began. I didn't want to lie. I wanted Miranda to like me for myself, and myself included a little spaceship and astronaut from Jupiter. Love me, love my nose.

But I didn't want her to think I was really weird. Funny was okay. Funny was nice. But really weird . . .

"Well," I said.

"Victor thinks it's all a big joke. You put on this funny ventriloquist act, and say all these outrageous things, but you're really you inside. Is that it?"

"I'm really me inside," I said. "That's for sure."

"And Norbert? Is Norbert real?"

"Well," I said. And then I felt a familiar little tickle at the back of my nose.

– Of course Norbert isn't real.

I frowned at the phone receiver. "You aren't?" I whispered. Norbert ignored me.

– Think about it, Miranda. A nose from Jupiter? Does that make sense? A nose with a spaceship, looking for a place to park? A nose drinking cocoa and playing soccer? Come on, now!

"I guess," Miranda said

– Norbert is just a part of Alan . . . the brave and funny part he's always had inside himself.

"You are?" I said.

– Shut up, you idiot, Norbert whispered.

"Who's an idiot?"

– You are!

Miranda laughed. "You're right, Squeaky. I should have known."

Before going to bed I turned out my light and stared out my window at Lake Ontario. We live across the street from the lake. The moon was almost full. The surface of the water looked like a black velvet garment with a swathe of shimmering sequins down the middle. Moon shadow made the place next door to ours look spooky. It isn't really spooky; it's very clean and squared off. An older couple lives there. At the end of the block is the funny family with all the little kids. Their place never looks spooky. The front lawn was covered in tricycles and basketballs as usual. She's a university professor and he's a – hard to say what he is, but he wears sweaters and laughs a lot and plays tag and baseball. And when one of the kids falls and gets hurt, he runs over and carries the injured one inside.

I was just about to pull the curtain when a movement in our garden caught my eye. I tried to look down, but couldn't because the angle was wrong. I was up too high and the garage overhang was in the way.

Had I imagined the shift of shadows by the big evergreen shrub? Had I?

Probably.

But I knew I wouldn't be able to sleep if I just ignored it. I'd be thinking about burglars trying to get in. Ugh. Walking downstairs in the dark was much scarier than I wanted it to be. I tiptoed to the bay window in the living room, and peered out at the garden. Was something moving around out there? Was someone? I couldn't be sure, shivering there in the dark, so I ran to the hall, switched on the outdoor floodlights, raced back to the living room, and *there* it was: a dark streak leaping into the shelter of the shadows. Was it a monster? A walking corpse? An emissary from the land of the undead? Was it a gopher? "Hey!" I shouted at the top of my lungs. The sound of my own voice was very loud in the silent nighttime house. I didn't want to go outside, but I wanted to see more if I could. I ran upstairs to my room and threw open the curtains.

There it was. Not a zombie. Not a gopher. A person.

A single figure, hunched over the handlebars, racing down the street and around the corner. The figure was dressed all in black, except for a familiar stencil on the back of the leather jacket. Too small to be one of the guys, or Mary. It had to be Prudence.

"Alan?" A muffled question from my mom's bedroom. "Were you shouting? Is everything all right?"

"Everything's fine," I said. "Sorry to wake you."

I went to bed, thoughtful. So the Cougars were spying on me, were they?

14

BAD OMEN

Next morning after breakfast I checked around the house. Sure enough, there was a set of strange footprints in the garden. They were human footprints and they were smaller than mine . . . about Prudence's size. One of the shrubs was knocked over, probably when she ran away. Of course it could have been one of the plants Victor and I trampled last week, playing football. I'm no Sherlock Holmes.

"Alan, what are you doing in the garden? You're getting your shoes all dirty." Mom was on the front step, frowning as she buttoned her coat over her new greeny-brown suit. Gee, this was only yesterday. Yesterday morning. It seems like a lifetime ago.

"Sorry," I said.

"I told you to keep those shoes clean. Your father will want you to look nice for the hockey game this weekend. He's always complaining that you dress like a tramp."

Thanks, Dad. "We're not going to the hockey game," I said. "Don't you remember? Dad phoned to say he can't make it."

Mom swore. I hate it when she does that because it's usually something to do with Dad. She slammed the car door and drove away, and I stopped trying to rub dirt off my desert boots.

I would have taken a lift with her except that her work is in the opposite direction from the school. I would have asked for a lift except that . . . I couldn't. If she said yes, I'd feel I was being a bother, and if she said no, I'd feel awful. It was better not to ask.

I walked to school very carefully. I didn't like the idea of Prudence in my neighborhood, watching my house. My house. (I thought of Cecil and his dirty pants.) I didn't like her standing in my garden, still as still, as the night came down. I didn't like her spying into my living room. My living room. I felt that something had been taken away from me. My life wasn't mine anymore.

I didn't see her – though I couldn't help feeling that someone was watching me, all the way to school. Once I looked over my shoulder and saw, or thought I saw, a shadow dart behind a tree. My heart did a somersault, and as I was about to scream and run away as fast as I could, a crow paced out from behind the tree and began, idly, to pull apart a piece of garbage with its sharp yellow beak.

Miss Scathely gave me my intramural championship ribbon in homeroom. Everyone applauded and I stuck it in my history textbook. Walking down the hall a few periods later, I ran into Prudence, who noticed the dangling ribbon and pulled it out.

"Very nice," she said tonelessly.

I thanked her.

"You could put it on the mantel in your living room," she said, "between that ugly horse statue and the clock that's five minutes slow." She handed back the ribbon and walked away.

I stared after her. She *had* been there. She knew what our living room looked like. My skin crawled as I imagined her standing in the garden, peering in through the window, noticing the carved, metal horse I'd bought my parents with allowance money, noticing that the mantel clock kept bad time. Who knew what else she'd seen?

But what could I do about it? I couldn't scare her away – I didn't think Dracula himself could scare Prudence. I sure couldn't intimidate her. Tell, no, *ask* her to stop spying on me? Great, and then I could run away, or stand there while she laughed at me or beat me to a pulp with or without the help of her friends. Not good options.

Miss Scathely couldn't help me – a teacher couldn't tell Prudence to stay out of my garden. Only the police could do that, and they wouldn't listen to a thirteen-year-old kid complaining about another thirteen-year-old kid.

I didn't get a chance to talk to Miranda until just before lunch, when we made our weekly visit to the school library. I started to tell her about Prudence, but she interrupted.

"I'm sorry for the way I sounded last night on the phone," she whispered. "Talking about you as if you were crazy. I hope you didn't take it too seriously. I was upset."

She took my hand. I said I understood. "Sh!" said the school librarian.

The janitor came in to empty the wastebaskets. I caught his eye by chance, and smiled politely. He stopped what he was doing and stared at me. I buried my head in my book.

"Something wrong?" asked Miranda in a whisper.

"Nothing."

After a long minute, the janitor shook his head and left. I drew a long breath.

"Why was Mr. Keenan staring at you?" Miranda asked.

I shook my head and turned a page of my book. Heaven knows what it was about. I hadn't read a word.

After the final bell I said good-bye to Miranda, who was waiting for her mom to drive her to a dentist's appointment. Saying good-bye must have taken longer than I realized because by the time I got to my locker, the usual crowd in the upstairs hall was thinning out. A knot of kids went by talking hockey. Another group went by talking hairstyles. Guys and girls. The girls couldn't decide whether the Avalanche were a better team than the Flyers. The guys agreed that a buzz cut was preferable to a skinhead – quite right too. Skinhead makes you look like a real jerk. I spun the combination lock on my locker to the right and stopped, to the left and stopped.

The sound of a toilet flushing echoed loud and long in the now empty hallway. The BOYS bathroom was two rooms away. For some reason, maybe remembering yesterday, I was suddenly filled with alarm. I hurried with the last number of my combination and couldn't get the lock to open. I took a deep breath and made sure the last number was right, but the lock still wouldn't open. I tugged and tugged, and then decided to start again.

I bent my head and spun the lock, but now everything I did seemed to be in slow motion, the way things happen in nightmares. Once around to the right and stop at –

Too late. The bathroom door opened and Victor came out.

"Hi!" I said in a too loud voice. I was probably more relieved than he was. My locker opened easily this time.

Victor looked up and down the hall before joining me. I asked if he wanted to walk home with me and he flinched, as if I'd offered him a live tarantula.

"No way," he whispered, hurrying into his coat. His eyes were wild.

"Why not?"

At that point the air near us was shattered by a resounding release of gas. Thunder on the right was a bad omen in ancient Rome, and also, it seemed, in present-day Ontario. Mary waddled up to us and stopped to stare at me for a moment.

I put on my coat and dumped my math homework into my knapsack. There are people who do badly in math because they never open the textbook. Not me. I manage to work hard *and* do badly.

Mary stared and stared. Her eyes – I'd never noticed before because I'd never been curious and close enough – were a pale blue, almost colorless. They regarded me with no apparent concern. I might have been a piece of meat on a slab. I might have been a booger on the end of her fingernail.

"There you are, Dingwall," she said. "We were wondering." I didn't reply. Mary turned and walked slowly down the hall, taking her own sweet . . . well, taking her own time. We watched her around the corner.

Victor shivered.

"Gotta go," he muttered. He patted my arm without looking at me, and hurried away in the opposite direction from Mary. Poor Victor. His head was bent forward. The bottom of his coat fit tightly across his rear end.

15

FALLING

The Cougars were playing catch near the north entrance. They all turned to stare at me when I came out of the school. Prudence wasn't with them, I noticed. Mary smiled when she saw me. I sneezed, and she laughed. Then she threw the football at Larry, hard and low. He dropped it. She laughed again. I joined the tail end of the stragglers who were leaving by the other gate.

I felt ashamed. I don't know why. I'd have left by the south gate normally.

I walked home alone. It was a cool and gray afternoon. The leaves had mostly fallen but were not raked up yet. They drifted about the front yards in clusters of red and gold. They clung to the moist pavement, making it slippery and colorful.

At the bottom of Forth Street, I turned right onto King. This part of town has some nice older houses, mostly falling down, and a few places that will fix your vacuum cleaner or your roof. Also a lumberyard and the newspaper offices and the water treatment plant. A mixed neighborhood, I guess you'd say. The few cars I saw in the parking lots were old and rusted. The sidewalks were empty.

I know the area well. I walk through it most school days. It's not so bad. Not friendly, exactly, but I'm used to it. You know how that is. You might not like the weird kid who lives on your block – the one who's always setting fires or teasing animals – but you're used to her.

Well, this afternoon, for some reason I found myself hurrying along King Street. I was scared. I wanted to get past the overgrown front lawns and boarded-up windows and rut-puddled driveways. I wanted to get to the other side of the river, where the houses start to get nicer and people are out walking. I didn't run, exactly, but I didn't waste any time. I didn't daydream either. I looked ahead, looked around, looked over my shoulder.

I didn't see anything strange, but I couldn't help the feeling that something was hovering nearby, waiting to leap out at me or drop out of the sky. Prudence in a black cape, maybe. I tried to laugh at myself but I wasn't feeling very funny.

I slipped on the pavement, went down on my backside, and scrambled up in a panic. No one was around. I was trembling. My heart was beating fast. Then I heard the noise – behind me. I turned. An old black car with a noisy muffler backed out of a beat-up driveway and turned to follow me.

I ran. I pumped my arms and legs and raced along the slippery sidewalk; my knapsack flapping heavily against my back. I wished I hadn't taken home my math book.

The car accelerated. It sounded like an airplane taking off. I ran harder. The bridge was over the next hill. I ran harder, harder, my shoes flapping, and the car got closer and closer and closer, and then it was too late.

The car caught up to me and passed. There was an old lady in the driver's seat; two hands on the steering wheel and a cigarette bobbing in the middle of her face. She smiled at me and took one hand off the wheel to wave. The car roared away.

I stopped running. Nothing had happened, except that I was sweaty.

"Norbert," I said. "I think I'm going crazy." He didn't answer right away. "Norbert, are you there?" After a minute he sneezed.

– *Excuse me. Of course I'm here. Where else would I be?*

"I feel a bit low. I might be getting a cold."

– *Take it from me. You are getting a cold.*

Your nose knows. "Miranda is going to ask her mom if I can come over for dinner tomorrow night."

– *She's at the dentist's, isn't she? She'll be able to pick some blossoms for the table setting.*

"What blossoms?"

– From the dentist-tree of course. We have them on Jupiter too. What an evocative smell. Crisp and minty. Now, Alan, what makes you think you're going crazy?

"Oh, I don't know. But talking to you isn't helping any."

The King Street bridge is nothing special – two lanes with a raised sidewalk and a tube-metal railing about chest high. Variety store and water treatment plant on one side of the water, nice houses on the other. In the summer the river is calm here, gentle crinkles of water between grassy banks. Shade trees lean over, dropping leaves to float downstream in slow and graceful eddies. You can count the stones in the riverbed, or watch the weeds waving a mournful good-bye to bubbles and ripples on their way downstream. I stopped in the middle of the bridge to catch my breath. The river was high and brown and busy; water churned past like a sinewy brown express train. Hard to believe it was just yesterday afternoon.

I crossed the bridge and was just about to push on when I saw the dog.

I'm sorry, my memory is getting faint here. I know there was a collie dog – the same one I had seen earlier at my house? Maybe. I can't say for sure. I have a picture of a tail wagging as the dog came running toward me – mouth open, tongue hanging out. I remember Norbert getting excited, yelling at the dog, telling me to get away; but the dog ran toward me, jumping up, barking wildly, and there was nowhere to go. I remember the dog leaping, and the river rushing by underneath the bridge. And then. And then.

And then I looked up. I saw the sky. I know I did.

Wait. It's coming back. The sky was moving fast, like the river, only the river was brown and the sky was gray with patches of blue. The river is getting closer, in my mind. I'm looking up at the sky but the river is getting closer. Behind me, the sound of the barking dog fades like music from inside a passing car.

I was falling. Is that why I looked up? I have a picture of the water coming up to meet me. Brown rushing water. And I remember a sensation of utter horror before I blacked out.

But it wasn't the water I was afraid of. I probably should have been afraid of it. Every year some kid falls into the river and drowns. They post signs and issue warnings on radio stations. We all get told in school to stay away from creeks and rivers when the water is high. I should have been afraid of drowning, of being swept away by the power of the water.

But I wasn't. There was something else. It was a voice. That's right, a voice right in my ear as I was falling. A voice I must have been expecting because I didn't feel surprise along with the horror. It gave a horrible little laugh, right in my ear, and I thought, 'Of course. Of course.' And I went under.

"Gotcha," it said, while I choked on dirty roaring water. "Gotcha now, Dingwall."

Prudence's voice.

16

PRUDENCE

My head aches. I'm hungry and thirsty, and I still have a stuffy nose. I reach across the hospital bed to the tray on wheels, and take a drink of ginger ale. Warm, of course, and a bit flat, but it feels good going down. I wonder when I get lunch.

My parents are still asleep. Stereo snoring. I yawn and wonder what time it is. It's bright outside. Going to be a sunny day.

Angela the nurse comes in with a smile, and asks me how I feel.

"Not bad," I tell her.

"You look better. Tina – that's the other nurse – says you didn't have too much pain. She says she wishes all her patients were as easy as you."

While Angela is talking, she's taking my temperature and blood pressure and neatening my bed. Nurses are like barbers, they can work and chat at the same time.

"Did you go to the bathroom?"

I nod my head. "All by myself."

"Any stools?" she asks.

"Huh?"

She explains. "In the bathroom. Did you just pee or did you –"

"Just pee," I said quickly. She's not embarrassed but I am. "I haven't eaten solid food in a long time."

"Didn't you get your snack? The doctor ordered it. Food services probably got mixed up." Angela looks at her watch and frowns. "Probably too late for snack now. I'm going to see what they have in the kitchens. Is that okay? Could you eat lunch if I got it for you?"

"Anything," I say, my mouth watering at the thought of stale hospital food. I must be getting better.

Angela takes blankets out of the closet and covers my sleeping parents. They're not her responsibility but she takes care of them. She's a nurse, she can't help herself. She goes out the door with a smile and a wave. A few minutes later I hear a cart with a squeaky wheel and my mouth starts watering. Pavlov's hospital patients.

But it isn't food. It's the lady who cleans. She nods at me, shakes her head at my parents, and empties the wastebasket. "Thank you," I tell her, but she's already out the door.

The next one who comes in is a doctor. I haven't seen this one before. "Hello, um, Alan," she says. "My name is

Doctor Mitchell." She doesn't look very old – more like a babysitter than a doctor.

"You must be tired," she says. I am tired but you know what? She's even more tired than I am. She looks enviously at my parents. She can't help yawning as she examines me. I don't have to take off my hospital gown, thank heavens. She puts the stethoscope down the front, and around the back. Then she stares into my eyes with the little flashlight. "Don't look at the light," she says, yawning. "Look beside it." I try.

When she's gone I lie back against the pillows and listen to my parents catch up on missed sleep. I'm lonely. I haven't heard from Norbert in awhile. I whisper his name but he doesn't answer.

Angela comes back with a tray. "The snacks were all gone," she says, "so I grabbed you an early lunch."

I thank her. Milk, ham sandwich with a sweet pickle for garnish, a muffin and, beside it, a bowl of – "What are those?" I ask.

"Prunes," she says.

I make a face. Pigeon eggs. Stool pigeon eggs. "Do I have to eat them?"

She shakes her head, and goes out the door with a smile. I push the bowl away. It's a great meal. The milk is warm and the pickle is rubbery but I don't care. I hardly notice. Food glorious food.

My parents wake up together. They say "Hi" to me, then, in quiet voices, with edgy politeness, begin to fight about who will go to the bathroom first. I try not to pay attention. I keep eating, but the food doesn't taste as good as it did a moment ago.

"I'm just fine," my dad says for the third or fourth time. "You go, dear. I know you want to comb your hair and freshen up for Alan."

"Thank you, dear, but really you're the one who should go. After all, you had to spend the night in the hospital."

"You had to drive to Cobourg and back. You must be exhausted. You use the bathroom."

"I'm feeling just fine, thank you."

My tray is empty, except for the prunes. I push it away. A doctor comes in. It's the one from yesterday, whose name I don't know. "Hi, Alan," she says. "How are you feeling?"

I tell her I'm feeling fine. "The food tasted great," I say.

"And how much do you remember about yesterday?"

I hesitate. "I can remember right up to the moment I fell in the water," I say, "but it's all a blank after that."

"That's great! I've known concussed football players who couldn't remember anything about the game. You remembered right up to the moment when you went unconscious. There may not be anything more to remember. By the time you got to the Cobourg Hospital, you were completely unresponsive. I have their report here."

I shake my head. It still hurts a bit. "I know there's something else," I say. "I can see – or almost see – an arm. And I can feel it pulling." It hurt, too.

The doctor nods. "Your girlfriend told the doctors that you were trying to speak when she pulled you out of the river, but I don't know how conscious you were. It might have been more like a dream."

Mom sniffs. Dad looks solemn. I frown, thinking about Miranda. There's something I've forgotten. I try to picture her pulling me out of the river, and I can't. There's a curtain between me and what happened yesterday. A curtain in my mind, and I can't tug it out of the way.

"I'm going to let you go home now," the doctor says. "This afternoon. Go home and rest. Can you promise to do that?" She looks at me and then at my parents. We nod. I don't know why Dad is nodding. I'm not going home with him.

The doctor holds up a cautioning finger. "No strenuous physical activities. I mean that. For the next few weeks, I don't want you involved in any contact sports. Do you understand, Alan? No climbing ladders or trips to Disneyland for awhile. And if you have any dizzy spells, vomiting, balance problems, go straight to hospital. Promise?"

I nod. She goes on. "I don't think you'll have any problems, though. I think you're fine. In the meanwhile," she smiles, closes my folder, "you can go home and get some sleep."

I'm still worried. Not about dizziness. "Doctor, will I ever get all the memory back?"

"There may not be much to get. You can't always remember a dream, even if it's a vivid one. And anyway, it's probably not a happy memory. You may be better off without it. I wish I could forget my last dentist's appointment." She smiles.

"That's it," I say.

"What?" She's startled.

"A dentist's appointment. Miranda had a dentist's appointment yesterday. She couldn't have walked home with me."

And at that moment there's a knock on the hospital door and Miranda walks in. But not by herself; Prudence is with her. Prudence, with her hair done up nicely under a little beret, and a clean leather jacket and blue jeans. She looks pretty. Even with the ring stuck in her eyebrow and a big wad of gum in her mouth, she looks pretty.

Miranda, of course, looks spectacular. Her eyes are swollen and her hair is uncombed and the collar of her jacket is all rucked up. Spectacular. "Alan," she says, running over to take my hand. "How do you feel?"

"Fine," I say.

"You didn't answer your phone last night. Prudence told me about your accident before school this morning and I . . . are you sure you're all right?"

Prudence stands there, hands on her hips, cracking her gum.

Mom stares at her. Not exactly friendly. Prudence ignores her. Dad straightens up to stand taller, and runs his hand over his hair to smooth it down. Prudence ignores him too.

My mother speaks to Miranda. "You must be the girl I spoke to on the phone. It's nice to see you, dear," she says. "I appreciate your concern for Alan's health. Where's your mother – parking the car?"

"No, Mrs. Dingwall." Miranda stands up straight. "Prudence and I – we came on the nine o'clock train from Cobourg."

I stare at Prudence. The curtain in my mind is slowly lifting. I can see bits of what happened yesterday. Prudence. Her hands, gripping tight; the muscles in her arms, bunching and pulling. Prudence.

My mom and dad are telling Miranda she shouldn't have come to a big city like Toronto by herself. Doesn't she know how dangerous it is? She's only thirteen years old. She should call her parents right away. They'll be so upset. And of course she'll have to come home with my mom and me.

No one seems too worried about Prudence. No one says she'll have to come home with us too.

Miranda smiles at my parents and doesn't say anything. In her own way, she's as tough as Prudence. A mind of her own. She squeezes my hand; I squeeze back. Meanwhile I'm thinking, no wonder my own arms feel like they've been dragged out of their sockets. No wonder I have bruises, not just from the rocks on the riverbed and the branches and stumps and rushing water, but from her incredibly strong hands.

Prudence saved me. The curtain across my memory has lifted and I can see now. I see her face an inch from mine, her hair dripping wet. I'm lying on the riverbank, coughing water. I remember Prudence covering me with her coat and going away. Getting smaller and smaller as she stood up, and then disappearing. And I disappeared too, and woke up in this hospital with my mom beside me.

I try to catch Prudence's eye, so I can thank her. She looks away.

The doctor is leafing through my file. "Prudence Armstrong," she says "you found Alan . . . is that right? And dragged him out of the river and called the ambulance?"

Prudence looks at her, nods.

"Pleased to meet you." They shake hands. The doctor waves good-bye to me and leaves the room.

My parents, thank heavens, stop talking. They stare at Prudence with open mouths and look embarrassed. I want them . . . I want my dad to thank Prudence. To say, "Thanks for saving my son." He doesn't.

But somebody should.

"Thank you, Prudence," I say.

She shakes her head. "Don't thank me. I didn't come here to be thanked."

"Why did you come here, then?" asks my mother.

"I came to apologize," says Prudence.

17

A MIRACLE ALL RIGHT

"Why?" We all ask it together but it's me she turns to.

"For following you around. For threatening to beat you up. For being a bully. I'm sorry, Alan. I've already spoken to the other Cougars. We won't bother you anymore. In fact, we won't bother anyone anymore."

Outside the old year is dying, getting ready for winter. Inside the hospital room, a new era is being born. I try to think of something mature and graceful to say. "Huh?" is what comes out.

She looks at the ground. "Well, Mary and Gary might still try to bother you. They're bad kids – the way I used to be. I told them they'd have to deal with me if they acted up – maybe that'll stop them. But they're bad kids. Mad and bad."

"Oh, the poor things," says Mom. Prudence stares at her.

"If it's not too difficult a question," I say, "how did you, er, decide to . . . well. . . ."

"To change my ways?" She smiles. Another difference. The old Prudence never smiled. "Is that what you are asking, Alan? What made me want to give up hurting people? Threatening them, making them scared? What made me want to become one of the good guys? Is that it?"

"Um, yes."

She looks serene and kind of thoughtful. "Would you believe I heard a voice from heaven? Speaking to me?"

Nobody says anything, and she goes on.

"I followed you home from school yesterday, Alan. On my bike. I'd done it for a couple of days. Did you see me last night, in your garden?"

I nod.

"I thought so. I took off pretty fast but I wondered if I'd been fast enough. Anyway, after school yesterday I rode over to the King Street bridge – that's the way you usually go home. I was inside the variety store there by the river, looking at a magazine, when I saw you come over the hill. I ran around the side of the store to get my bike, and that's when you fell in."

My mom whispers, "Oh no. Oh no."

"I didn't fall. I tripped over that dog."

"Yes. The collie dog." She frowns. "She isn't *your* dog, is she, Dingwall? I never thought of that."

"No," I say. "Not my dog."

"She didn't have a collar, you see."

133

A cart squeaks down the hallway and enters the room. The guy pushing it is an orderly – not the one from this morning. He takes away my empty lunch tray. Prudence goes on.

"I ran over to the water. I don't know what I was going to do. I was kind of glad that you'd got in trouble." She turns to me, blushing. Another first. "I'm sorry, but I was. I said to myself, 'Yes! He's got what's coming to him!' I felt powerful, like I was calling down vengeance from the sky to punish you for bad-mouthing me and my team, and breaking Gary's nose."

"Alan?" says my mom, displeased. "Did you break some-body's nose?"

"Son?" says my dad. I can't tell if he's pleased or not.

I shrug my shoulders.

"You were lying in the water," says Prudence, "and you started to drift away. And then I heard a voice. I don't know how I knew it was an angel, but I did. 'Save him,' said the angel." She's smiling, reliving the memory.

I can think of only one explanation. "Did the angel have a high, squeaky voice?" I ask.

"No," says Prudence. "It was a deep voice. And it was right beside me, warm and strong and sort of – wet. Very alive! I never thought angels would sound so alive. Almost in my ear. 'Save him and save yourself.' And it called me by name. 'Save yourself, Prudence.' I don't know what I was saving myself from. I turned my head and there was the collie dog. Are you sure she's not yours?"

"Not mine," I say. "All I do is trip over her."

"But," Miranda frowns at Prudence, "are you saying — was it the *dog's* voice you heard? Warm and wet and all? The dog is really an angel?"

"I don't know," says Prudence. "I only know I heard it."

Standing there beside me, a suddenly nice girl. Prudence. It's a miracle all right.

"Anyway, before I really understood what I was doing, I was running downstream and wading out to grab you."

The bruises on my arms throb with recollected pain.

"Thanks," I say again. This time my parents say "Thank you" too. Prudence looks away. My dad goes over and holds out his hand. Prudence's grip makes him wince.

Angela the nurse comes in without a thermometer or blood pressure gauge. Almost like she's naked. At least she's got a clipboard. "There are a couple of forms to fill out," she tells my parents. "Then Alan can go home." They follow her out the door to fight over which one of them ought to sign the forms. My dad is still wiggling the fingers of his right hand.

"Your folks are okay," Prudence says to me. Does she mean it? I've never met her folks. If she means it, I don't think I want to meet her folks.

"Do you guys believe in my angel?" Prudence asks us.

I don't know what to say.

"I believe in voices," I say. "Sometimes I hear them too."

She nods. "It's funny that you should ask about a squeaky voice, just now. Because when I got you onto the bank, I tilted you on your side, and all this water poured out of your nose and mouth. And a different voice – a high, squeaky voice – said, 'Thank you.' At first I thought it was you, Dingwall. You know when you talk without moving your lips? But I called your name and you didn't say anything. So then I thought I was going crazy, hearing voices where there weren't any. I got mad for a moment. That voice reminded me of you insulting me at the soccer game. I actually thought about tipping you back in the river, only, of course I couldn't. Not after having pulled you out."

"No," I say faintly.

"So maybe it was another angel talking to me."

"Maybe. Or a nose."

"What was that?" she asks.

"I said, who knows?"

The girls leave the room while I get changed. Mom has a knapsack full of clean clothes from home, including clean underwear. Blue this time, if you're interested. It's a sunny, windy day – I can tell from the window of my room, which overlooks the dumpster, by the way. I don't know why everyone kept staring out at it last night.

Mom has decided that we will all go home to Cobourg together. Me, her, and the girls.

Not Dad. He has to get back to his meeting in Vancouver. "I'll get back here soon," he says. "Maybe we can see a hockey game. Or basketball. Do you follow basketball?"

"Sometimes," I tell him. We're standing outside in a windy parking lot. The girls are already sitting in the backseat of the car. Mom is standing by the driver's side, staring at us. The wind is whipping at her coat.

"Well, Alan, I'm glad you're feeling better. I was really worried, you know," he tells me.

"Yeah," I say.

We stare at each other for a minute. My mom calls to me to hurry up.

"Well – bye, son," says my dad. He holds out his hand, kind of tentatively, and puts it on my shoulder. After a minute he takes it off and turns to walk away. He's not going to say he misses me, or thinks about me, or loves me. He's not going to say any of those things.

Prudence is right. He's okay. But is that all he is? Okay? Shouldn't a parent be more than that? Shouldn't your dad be more than just, okay?

"I love you, Dad," I say, but the wind whips my words away. He doesn't hear me, doesn't turn around.

18

A FORGOTTEN VOICE

For a week my head aches under the bandage. I rest at home, surrounded by pillows and CDs and rental movies. Victor drops by most days after school to tell me how much homework I'm going to have to do when I finally get back. Mrs. Grunewald comes all the way down the street from her house to tell me I'm a sweet boy, and to leave off a cake she made herself. Miranda phones every evening. Not a bad life, if it weren't for the headache, and even that goes away in time. When the bandage finally comes off, I'm as good as new.

I stare at myself in the bathroom mirror. Wednesday afternoon. I'll be going to school tomorrow. Only two days left in the week. My head is smaller than I'm used to, without the layers of white wrapping. My hair has grown a bit and is sticking out all over the place. Serious case of bed-head. And I look – I don't know how to put it – older. I know I am older, a whole week older, but what I mean is I look older than that . . . like I'm almost grown-up . . . like I'm ready to start driving and shaving and worrying about a job. It's the eyes, mostly. They look as if they've seen a lot of stuff.

Then my mom knocks and comes in. She kisses the top of my head. "Feeling better, my little honey bun?" she says, like she used to when I was small.

"Uh huh," I say.

"It's nice to see you without that ugly bandage. Why don't you wash your hair? Shall I run you a bath? Maybe with some bubbles?"

"Okay," I say.

"You could play with the plastic frog that swims all the way across the bathtub."

"Okay," I say. Maybe I don't look much older to Mom.

"Remember to rinse thoroughly," she says.

I get out of the bath, put on clean clothes, come downstairs. Mom is putting on her coat. "I have to go to the office for a bit. Are you going to be okay on your own?"

That's what she always says – "a bit." "I'll be gone for a bit." "I'll be ready to go in a bit." "I'll be back in a bit." Sometimes a bit is an hour, sometimes more. When she promised to sew my torn blue jeans, a bit was two months.

"Sure," I say.

There's something I've been meaning to do. Five o'clock in Cobourg is two o'clock in Vancouver. I phone my dad at work. I want to make this a business call.

I've given it a lot of thought. I can't change the way Dad and Mom feel about each other. I can't expect them to wake up and like each other, suddenly – to move back together so I can have real parents again, and it'll be like it was before Dad left. I can't change the people they are. I can't turn my dad into an affectionate, loving father. He's okay. He cares for me. He's all the dad I'm going to get.

I can't make him give me a hug, but there's one thing I can do. I can tell him how much he means to me, how much I love him. If he were around I could do it in person. But he's almost never around. He's a long-distance dad, so I'll do it over the phone. And I'll do it now, because if I put it off, he'll only move farther away.

"Hello," I say into the phone. "Could I please speak to my dad?"

"One minute. I'll transfer you." That's Mrs. Hertz, his secretary. I've met her. Her nose twitches all the time. I take a deep breath and press the phone into my ear.

"Is that you, son?" my dad asks.

"Yes, Dad."

"Alan?" Like he has a lot of other sons.

"None other," I say.

"Is something wrong? You okay? And your mom?"

"Everything's fine, Dad. How are things with you?"

"Fine, fine. Can't complain. Well – gosh. You sound so

grown-up. How are you doing? How's Helen? Gee, son, it's nice to hear your voice."

"Yours too, Dad."

"And I'd love to, uh, keep talking to you, Alan. But I've got a meeting in a few minutes. This is a working day, you know. So I'm afraid –"

"Wait!" I shout it into the phone.

Silence.

"Before you hang up, Dad. Just let me say: I love you."

Silence.

"There. That's all."

Silence.

"See you sometime. Bye, Dad."

"Wait!" Now he sounds agitated.

"Yes, Dad?"

"Wait a second. I love you too, son. I hope you know that. You're my son and I will always love you. Do you know that?"

"Sure, Dad."

"I'm sorry I live so far away. Your mom and I . . . well, we don't get along, but that's not your fault. It's our fault. When you're older you'll understand more."

"Sure, Dad. I don't mean to put you on the spot there at work. I wanted to tell you how much I love you at the hospital, but I felt lousy and there never seemed to be any time. Now I'm feeling better. In fact, I go back to school tomorrow."

"That's great, son. Just great. I'm pleased. Make sure you treat those girlfriends of yours nicely – the ones who came up to see you on the train. They seem to like you a lot."

"Yeah. Uh. I have to go now, Dad." I can feel the skin of my face tightening as it gets hotter and redder. I suppose it's only fair. I embarrassed him. Now it's his turn to embarrass me.

"I'm glad you called, son. Maybe you could do it again sometime."

"Maybe," I say, and we hang up together, both of us knowing I'm not going to call again, and he's not going to be too disappointed.

When Mom comes back from work, she wonders if I'm feeling all right. I look a little feverish, she says. My eyes are red and swollen.

I tell her I'm okay.

I make sure I'm early when I call on Victor the next morning. I don't want to be late my first day back to school. It's a crisp clear morning, sun glinting off the frost. We haven't had snow yet, but you know it's coming soon. Victor's mom won't let me walk. "Whatever are you thinking of, you foolish child?" she says, but in a nice tone of voice. She stands at the door, and drifting out from the kitchen is a smell I know well, a bewitching scent of blueberry pancakes. "Of course you'll take a ride with my man. He'll be leaving in a few minutes, so you've time to step in for a bite."

Victor and his dad are eating and arguing. There's a platter of pancakes in the middle of the table, and a pitcher of syrup, and a clean plate for me. "Thanks," I say to Mrs. Grunewald. Captain Crunch isn't bad, but it doesn't compare with homemade pancakes. "Thanks a lot."

Mr. Grunewald wants Victor to come and work at the store after school. They need people to help bag the groceries and move stock around. "Come on. It's a great opportunity for you," he says. "It'll only be for a few weeks around Christmastime, when we're really busy."

Victor doesn't want to do it. "Oh, Dad. I hate working at the store. You have to wear a dumb apron, and those vegetables really stink."

"I don't know, Vic. Sounds good to me," I say with my mouth full of pancake.

"There, see. Our friend Alan here thinks it's a good idea."

"Then let him do it," says Victor. "I don't want to smell like onions."

Mr. Grunewald pushes away his plate. Time to go.

I stand up. "Actually, I kind of like the smell of onions," I say.

Mr. Grunewald considers me for a moment, then gets up from the table to put his hand on my shoulder. "Good for you," he says.

Then we all pile into the delivery truck and drive to school.

I never knew so many people liked me. The school yard is full of people when we arrive, and it seems like they all come over to shake my hand or clap me on the back. They're all glad to see me – not just my class, but kids I barely even know, kids I've seen in the cafeteria, at the candy store, at the mall. I'm a celebrity. Reminds me of the guy last year who fell while he was hiking in the woods, and was found two or three days later, alive but with a broken leg. A Grade Eight guy. I signed his cast – along with everyone else. I've already forgotten his name.

Miranda holds my hand – an experience which is somewhere between very nice and very embarrassing. No one laughs, I notice. Prudence smiles, but not at us holding hands. She smiles because her stupid dog jumps up on me and licks my face, and I stumble and almost fall down.

Already the smile is looking as if it belongs on Prudence's face. "I've named her Angel," she tells me. The collie keeps jumping up at me. "Down, Angel," says Prudence. The dog ignores her and keeps jumping up and down. Everyone thinks it's a riot.

"Help," I say. "Get her off me!" The dog won't leave me alone. Miranda and Prudence are talking together, ignoring me. Where is Vic? "Help," I say again.

And I hear, for the first time in awhile, a small high voice I'd forgotten about.

– *So you* do *need me after all!*

19

IT'S TIME

"Norbert!" I say.

– You were expecting Peter Pan?

"Where've you been?" I can't say I've actively missed Norbert – my life has been full of stuff to do, hardly enough time to think let alone have a conversation with your nose – but I have wondered. I used to hear his voice as often as my own. I was used to him shocking people or making them laugh, getting me in trouble by saying things I'd never dream of saying. But it seems I've hardly heard from him since I left hospital.

– I've been right here. If you want to know, I've been packing.

"You're not leaving?"

– I've been thinking about it.

"Not back to Jupiter?" My heart sinks. I feel strangely sad, thinking of life without Norbert. The dog jumps up again. "Ugh!" I say, my face covered in dog tongue.

– *I haven't decided. I could go back home, I suppose. But I've been scanning the HELP WANTEDS. There are a lot of people out there who need help, you know. More than you need it, now – Hey! Angel! Down, girl! Sit and stay, already!*

You know what? The dog sits and stays. Probably something to do with Norbert's voice. Dogs respond to high-pitched sounds, don't they?

Prudence stops talking to stare at me. "How do you get her to obey you?" she says in a tone of admiration. I've never heard that before.

"Way to go, Squeaky!" says a girl named Tiffany. I don't know her very well.

In the middle of the playground, hunched into an under-sized leather jacket against the cold, I see Mary. She's leaning against the sick elm tree, peering over at us. And for just a second, from this distance, I catch a look of – can it really be – longing, on her face. She's all by herself and she wants – or part of her wants – to belong. She wants people to like her.

The bell rings. Time to line up. "Go home, Angel," says Prudence, giving the dog a little pat on the flank. She stays put.

I get in line. A guy I've never spoken to before, a basket-ball player with pale pink hands and a face like the surface of the moon, asks how I am doing. His Adam's apple bobs like a cork when he talks. He is so thin you could push him in the middle and he'd fold in half, like a lawn chair. "I'm fine," I tell him.

"Good. My name's Quincy," he says.

I know. In a small town you know everybody. Quincy and I have never been introduced, but I know everything about him. He's got a younger sister and two younger brothers, and his parents are divorced like mine. "Hi," I say. "I'm Alan."

"I know," he says. See. He knows too.

Gary the bully walks past me. His nose is a different shape than it used to be. And it's all my fault. I feel a small twinge of shame and a big prickle of apprehension. I wonder if he's ready to forgive and forget. Let bygones be bygones. Shake hands and forget about the past.

Gary butts in front of me. COUGARS on the back of his jacket. The tall, skinny basketball player, Quincy, doesn't move out of the way fast enough. Gary pushes him in the stomach – not that hard, but sure enough, Quincy folds up.

My little twinge of shame goes away. My apprehension grows. "Hey," I say. Gary turns around to glare at me. Pretty good glare he's got. The broken nose helps, too. He steps on my toe. Deliberately. With heavy boots. The line moves forward. The basketball player straightens himself up again, and shuffles ahead, leaning like tall grass in the wind. Gary grinds my foot, stepping close to me, staring into my face. Probably not ready to forgive and forget, just yet. Maybe next week. Maybe next year. Maybe after he's killed me a couple of times.

Ouch.

I can hardly walk when he finally lifts his foot. I find myself looking around for Prudence, but she and Miranda are over by the fence, motioning for Angel to go home.

"Move along there," says a teacher.

I'm hobbling. The line hurries past me. Mary catches up. When she sees me limping, she chortles meanly. Saliva bubbles at the side of her mouth. Maybe I was wrong about Mary. Maybe she doesn't want to be liked. If she does, she's sure going about it the wrong way.

"What's wrong, Squeaky?" Miranda asks, when she catches up to me. "Is your head bothering you?"

"Not my head," I say.

My class gives me an ovation when I come in. I can't help wondering if Prudence's class gives her an ovation. She's the hero, not me. All that happened to me is that I fell in the water and got knocked unconscious. She pulled me out. There's nothing special about being a victim. Anyone can do it.

But it's nice to see your friends clapping for you, wishing you well, glad to see you back. Victor makes the long ceremonial trip from Miss Scathely's desk to mine, bearing in his arms an incredible mountain of – yes – homework. I wish he didn't look so pleased with himself.

And then it's back to business as usual. Flora and fauna. *Je suis, tu es, il est*. The War of 1812. I'm not looking forward to the next few days, getting caught up to all this.

By lunchtime everything is normal. I might never have

been away. Victor and Dylan and I are sitting at our usual table, trading sandwiches around. Dylan actually likes cheese spread – can you believe it? On Wonder bread. I'm happy to trade for his mom's roast beef on dark rye, with barbecue sauce. A couple of tables over, Prudence is talking to the girl who used to get teased for dressing like a boy. I know it's stupid to make fun of the way people dress, but it happens. I suppose it's stupid to make fun of people, period. Miranda comes in late, smiles at me, and then goes over to her usual table.

All very normal. Close my eyes and it might be the first week of school – before the hospital, before the assembly, before intramurals. Before Norbert.

I'm going to have to find out what's going on with him.

Great news! Mr. Duschene, the math teacher, is away with the flu. His replacement is a kindly old lady who uses a big cardboard clock-face to explain about different bases in a way that I can – this is hard to believe – understand. She asks a question in base seven and I quick-draw the answer as fast as Billy the Kid. Faster than Victor, who turns around in his seat to stare at me. I examine my fingernails like I do this all the time. Nothing to it. Base seven – huh!

Toward the end of the period she puts a question on the board, and the answer simply *flashes* into my head. Incredible. I feel like Galileo or somebody; or I do until the teacher works out the answer on the board. Not my answer – a different one. Hmm. She writes down another question, and the same thing happens. Another question – and another mistake. And another. That first correct answer must have been a fluke. Even a stopped clock tells the right time once every twelve hours. Drat.

The bell rings. Last bell. The near-silent classroom erupts into a sudden busy clatter of slammed books, pushed-back chairs, and raised voices.

My knapsack weighs a ton. I'm walking down the stairs by myself. Victor has disappeared. People say "Hi" to me, and then dash away. I get to the school yard alone.

The two remaining Cougars are at the south gate. Mary and Gary. They're both bigger than I am, meaner than I am.

The school population is filing toward the north gate.

I head across the school yard all by myself, against the traffic flow. More people say "Hi," then stop to watch me. I head for the south gate.

I wonder where Prudence is. I look around for Miranda, but the bus has already left. Prudence could be anywhere, off trying to get that dumb dog of hers to do something. I'm all alone, walking across the school yard toward the bullies.

I feel like a western hero. I should have a gun belt and a cowboy hat, instead of a knapsack and a toque.

Mary is smiling. Not nicely. Not like she's going to invite me to play with her.

"Hey, Dingwall!" she shouts. "Come on and get your –" Well, I won't say what she says, but it's not very nice. Nothing I haven't heard before, but not very nice at all.

I keep going. I don't know why – it's something I have

to do. Still, I wish I weren't alone. Prudence would be a good ally, but she's not around.

It would be great if the other kids in the playground took heart from my example, and lined up behind me so that we all turned on the bullies together. Very inspiring, that.

Doesn't happen.

The kids in a hurry to get home keep walking. The rest hang back, watching. I don't think they want to see me bleeding, but they aren't going to join my crusade.

"I wish I weren't alone," I murmur, walking closer and closer.

– *You're not*, comes the familiar voice.

"I mean, I wish I had some real help," I say.

– *You have all the help you need*, Norbert tells me. Gee, he sounds serious. Ordinarily he'd make a smart answer.

An early winter afternoon. Gray sky, with the sun poking through every now and again, a pale milky thing already halfway down the west.

"Where do you think you're going, Dingwall?" calls Gary.

"Home," I say. No muss, no fuss. Making my way toward the gate.

"The way out is over there," Mary says, pointing. A kid in the middle of the school yard thinks she's pointing at him, turns his back and starts walking away.

"I want to go out this way," I say in a quiet voice.

"Well you can't!"

They stand near the gate, ready to block it. I look over my shoulder.

Mary laughs. "No one coming to help you, Dingwall. Not even your new friend Prudence. She's in detention for another forty minutes."

"You'd better go out the other side, with everyone else," says Gary.

– *Good-bye, Alan,* Norbert whispers to me.

"What? You're going now?"

– *It's time.*

I stop. Mary and Gary step toward me.

"Gee, Norbert, I don't know what to say. Good luck."

– *Thank you. Good luck to you too.*

Gary and Mary have big happy grins on their faces. They're going to enjoy beating me to a pulp.

"Will I ever hear from you again?"

– *Of course.*

"How will I know you're there?"

– *You'll have to listen. If you listen hard, you'll hear me. I'll be around.*

"Oh." I take a deep breath. Gary and Mary are almost up to me now. Hero time. I wonder what the pavement feels like. I expect I'll find out, soon enough. I keep walking.

– *Remember. You're not alone.* It's the last thing he says.

"What was that, Dingwall? You trying to squeak something at us?" says Mary.

Gary stops, momentarily uncertain. The last time he heard Norbert's voice was in the bathroom, just before he got his nose broken.

The gate is ten steps away. I'm scared, but I don't want to turn around and go back across the school yard. I don't even want to dash past Mary and Gary and on out the gate. I want to walk out.

I'm close enough to smell Mary's breath – not minty and fresh. She reaches out her hand toward my throat. I don't say anything witty. I don't say anything.

What I do, I sneeze.

Some sneezes are dry and polite, little snorts really, so restrained that they're easy to miss. More of the sneeze is inside than outside. Like a cap pistol that misfires, all you hear is a little fizz and a click. And some sneezes are neither dry, nor polite, nor easy to miss. The sneeze I give in front of Mary and Gary is warm and wet and explosive, a real elephant gun of a sneeze. I get pushed backward by the force of the recoil.

Mary covers up like she's been shot, which of course she has. She screams and takes an involuntary step back. I move forward and fire again. And again. And keep walking. My head hurts. My ears are ringing. The air is filled with – well, not smoke.

"Geez, Gary, what is that?" Mary's voice seems to come from a long way away.

"Watch out! It's coming after us!"

My eyes are a little blurry, you know how it is when you sneeze really hard. There's a little dark speck hovering in front of Mary and Gary, flitting back and forth like a horsefly.

They back away – away from me and away from the gate. The speck – it flashes gold, for just a second, as the sun peeps through a hole in the afternoon cloudbank – the speck follows them, darting between them, driving them away.

I wonder. I take a deep breath in through my nose. It feels the same inside, but I wonder.

"Norbert?"

No answer.

"Norbert? You there?"

Silence. I listen hard, but all I hear is silence.

"Well, thanks," I say.

Then I hitch up my knapsack and walk through the south gate.

20

HE'S OKAY

Just a couple of more things to say. I take the job at Safeway, working for Mr. Grunewald. Mom does her shopping there, stopping in on her way home from work. Usually I'm finishing my shift about then, so I get a lift with her. I end up seeing more of her, not less. Also it means I can help with the shopping. We haven't had rice, or chicken tenders, in awhile.

I'm supposed to go to the hospital in Toronto again next month, for another MRI test. My nose feels the same as always, but somehow I doubt that they'll be able to see a mysterious spaceship shape inside the garage part of my nose.

Mom asks how my imaginary friend is doing. When I tell her he seems to be gone, she nods her head. "It's all part of growing up, Alan," she says.

"I miss him, sometimes," I tell her. "I hope he's okay."

"I'm sure he's fine," my mom says.

And she could be right. A few days later I'm at Miranda's for dinner, again – yes, I've been over a few times now – and we're sitting on the couch afterward, watching a country music special on TV. Live from the Rose Bowl or someplace. Someplace warm and outside. k.d. lang is onstage, singing about a big-boned girl, smiling but bothered by . . . well, on TV it sure looks like an insect. You can see it in the spotlight, following her around the stage. She's shaking her head back and forth, and waving her hands. Suddenly there's a screech; sounds like feedback noise from the microphone. Anyway, k.d. stops for a second, recovering herself. And when she goes on singing, she's distracted. You can see it because the camera is right in her face. Her nose . . . I'll swear her nose is twitching.

At the end of the song, the crowd goes wild. k.d. takes a handkerchief out of her pocket. We go to a commercial about laundry soap.